CHECKING OUT
An In-Depth Look at Losing Your Mind

by Catherine Graves

Life is mostly froth and bubble;
Two things stand like stone—
Kindness in another's trouble,
Courage in our own.

Adam Lindsay Gordon (1833-1870)

Acknowledgments

My thanks to Tom Hughes, who collaborated with me on my story. He was able to ask the right questions and provide the right research to help turn my manuscript into an actual book.

To my publicist, Lauren Rosenberg. Without her, my manuscript would still be sitting inside of my computer waiting to be told.

Gretchen Perry, my best friend. She has been there for every hardship, for every twist and turn my life has taken. She is my rock.

To Ali Hudak and Sheryl & Mark Jones, for being there for me when I needed them most.

John's children, Erinn, Clinton and Riley Graves, for their loving support of their father.

Thanks to my parents, David Charak and Diane Freyman, for giving me stability and strength during this trying time when I've needed it most.

My counselor and friend, Sarah Matheson, for holding me back from the ledge.

My girlfriends, Mary Kincaid, Karen Bolwar and Betsy Serrano. Thanks to them for keeping me laughing practically every morning during our "coffee talks" long after John passed away. Laughter is indeed the best medicine.

To my neighbors, Stephanie and Ryan O'Donovan. They were there for me anytime I needed a break, ready with a glass of wine, and willing to hear me "whine."

Lori Mandino, for being better than the "sister" I never had.

My dear friend, Christina Decker, who never stops believing in me.

৵৽

Dedication

To my beautiful and loving children, Alex & Caroline, truly the joys of my life, who have been patient and supportive throughout this entire process. You light up my world everyday and have always been my greatest teachers.

To my late husband, John Graves, who comes to me as a stunning butterfly in my dreams.

And to Dante Graves, John's son and my stepson. I'm grateful that you came into my life and the lives of my children.

తిం ఆం

I also wish to thank the following groups of people who helped get me through each day:

The staff and counselors at Psychological Counseling Services, for making what could have been a daunting experience one of the best of my life. So much so that I didn't want to leave.

The faculty, clergy and community of All Saints' Episcopal Day School and Church, who have shown me for the first time in my life what "community" really means.

The nurses and volunteers at Hospice of the Valley's Sherman Home. They are truly all angels sent from heaven. The acts that they perform are without a doubt miraculous.

తిం ఆం

Prologue

There never will be a shortage of sad stories. At least twice as many as there are people in this world, more than double the measure most people want to be told. But they're not trackers or stalkers or paid-for followers you can elude by crossing a street and melting into the flowing crowd. The crowds, of course, are where the stories live, and there is nowhere you can walk where you won't catch even the faint tone of one in the air. There's no home too humble or elegant that doesn't hold its roof over a narrative, tender and agonized. You are, each of us is, one of these people, the title-holder of one of these tales. Don't be so surprised when you find one day that that barely detectable quaver in a voice heard in a fine room is the small, unintended weakness in your own. I was. And by the time I recognized that voice was mine, I felt I'd made every mistake, accepted every bad decision, taken every wrong step one could and still be alive to tell my tale.

But I was wrong about that. About the seeming irreversible, irretrievably downbeat qualities of life. I am alive. I am well. And I have learned an important hard-won truth. I didn't ask for this knowledge, expertise no one in her right mind would ever want to earn. But I did earn it, and once received one has to decide exactly what to do with it: bury it so deep that you never hear its echo again or use it to reinvent a life moving forward and offer that knowledge to those in need so their lessons don't need to be so grueling.

I worked for my education, boiled it down, and I'm going to use it. One true thing I found during that process kept rising to the surface, and it can be expressed this way: When you're losing someone you love, when you're on the narrow ledge of losing yourself, when you see someone else balancing on that same edge, stay true to yourself, let good people help keep you on the path of your life. From your loved ones, your reliable friends, your newest honorable intimates, and above all from that truest center of yourself, never walk away.

Part One
Life'll Kill Ya

1.

To borrow, and revise for my purposes, a classic Zen koan: What is the sound of one man dying? Not the environment around the event, which can be anything from earsplitting to unearthly silent, but the sound of life's final task itself? It is simply the sound of a single outward breath, then the absent sound of the next breath never taken.

I heard that lost sound from my husband, John, a man I'd loved truly and whose life I'd fought for, on a day he would have treasured living through: 7-07-007. He was the most loyal of James Bond fans, and had he been aware of the date he might have fought through it to show his favorite superspy just how tough he could be. He might have been able to conjure one last, great big broad smile on his handsome face. But instead there was only the final great hush of that never-to-be-found breath. To the outside things were now profoundly silent, but my head was filled with such a cacophony of memories and fears and sorrow that there wasn't room enough even for the smallest echo of what I'd just seen happen. The dénouement to eleven months of inexplicable behavior, misunderstood motives, weeks of confusion and fear, which had led to the last thing John and I had ever expected: the diagnosis of a brain tumor of the worst kind, a glioblastoma multiforme. Absolutely incurable and promising an arduous lifetime of less than a year to the injured party, in this case John, who had undergone profound personality and intellectual changes in a few months time without even perceiving them.

The story of John's illness is obviously the most tragic episode of our story together, and of my life—no matter how inexplicable—after John. But it's not where or how our lives began, and I would come to realize that it's not where it ended either. So here, a short history of how John and I met, what our lives were, and the first hints of how we would be transformed by the coming unpredictable experience.

This is not "Cinderella" or "Sleeping Beauty"; it's not even "Shrek." (Is there anyone whose life is close to reflecting any fairy tale, no matter how happy or Grimm?) John had been married twice before we'd met, and I was on my way out of a marriage that felt like the gears were all trying to work in opposite directions.

John had three children with his first wife. John's second wife—who had a son from a previous marriage whom John adopted—had died tragically from an accidental overdose of prescription medications. (Her son, Dante, had found her, a devastating experience from which he has courageously lifted his life.)

With my first husband I had the great fortune to have two wonderful children, Caroline and Alexander. And so when John and I met it wasn't like we were two naive souls hovering in the ether for the perfect partner. More like two slightly disheveled travelers at Sky Harbor Baggage Claim, both a little overwhelmed by what we'd already plucked from the eternal luggage carousel and watching for the next recognizable kit to appear at the top of the ramp and tumble down at our feet, nametags torn but too familiar to let them pass by.

We met purely by chance while we were working at a fundraiser for Phoenix Children's Hospital. And then just like that it was "Cinderella" and "Sleeping Beauty"(and maybe a little "Shrek") rolled into one. John was handsome. He stood at almost six foot five inches tall, with piercing blue eyes and a full head of hair. The best part about this was his lack of awareness of just how handsome he was. It wasn't that he was being modest—he genuinely didn't consider how good looking he really was. John was a wonderful husband and partner. He was the yin to my yang. We were operating on the "opposites attract" theory, but we had enough in common where it counted. We were each swept up by the other in the sweetest of ways, a twist of luck and fate neither of us imagined possible anymore. True romance. Not road-weary tourists, but two people renewed by each other and joyously in love. And so we married, knitted our respective families together as neatly as we could, and began an inspired new life.

We went into business. We were living in Phoenix, John having moved back from Albuquerque. He had been running his own company there, but decided to come back to Phoenix to work in his family's concern. With the Arizona building boom rolling along fast, furiously, and with a sense of the inevitable like a shopping cart toward a showroom-new Bentley, we decided to start Villa Pavers, a paver-stone installation company. It was right in tune with John's family business of manufacturing supplies for the building trades. Most importantly, John and I would be working shoulder-to-shoulder (or in this case, stone-by-stone) and building our future together. It was exciting. A terrific feeling. Creating a practical, profitable venture together was something we'd hoped we could do, and now we were doing exactly that. The bubbles in our champagne.

But those bubbles are born to burst, given time, just like all bubbles. As it turned out (and the truth of this became obvious not long after we'd started our business) John and I had very different work philosophies and ambitions. John was, if this isn't too much of an oxymoron, intensely laid-back; I'd have to describe myself as somewhat more driven. Those two divergent styles might accomplish something in certain situations: in a squad car with one good cop, one bad. A pair of comics, one straight man, the other all punch lines, has worked nicely from the earliest days of theatre right up to today's "YouTube" comics. But in a relatively modest-sized business as practical and competitive as was ours, and with profit margins that had to be hawk-watched, there wasn't room for a good paver guy/bad paver girl scenario. The business required that we both work with maximum efficiency, watching every nickel that went out the door and every dime that came back in.

But it wasn't working out that way.

John was easygoing to a fault, more apt to let an invoice go unmailed or unpaid for a time if, for instance, a customer was having cash-flow problems. I knew that if that mindset became officially unofficially formalized with our customers, we'd soon enough be in the same predicament as those customers. And the dream of our working together, that perfect bubble, began to wobble and weaken a bit in the breeze. Though it would be the source of some tensions addressed and suppressed in our lives, it did not ever burst with destructive force. Regrettably, that would come with other events.

While John may have lacked the naked desire of a covetous tycoon, he was the best father any child could hope to have. This was the man that brought tradition and value into our home. He taught Caroline how to make Chocolate Chip Pie (much to my dismay) at their first Thanksgiving so that she would know how to make it every year. He was always full of fun family surprises. Each year he purchased Christmas pajamas and gave them to all of us on Christmas Eve. We would them drive around town to the houses with the best light displays that he had spent the afternoon mapping out, with the kids in the back of the car, sipping on hot chocolate and eating their popcorn. It was impossible to resent what I may have seen as John's entrepreneurial shortcomings whenever I saw or pictured him playing with our created and collected "works."

John was patient, tireless, always available to the children for any problem, any party, any kind of play he or they could imagine. He was their Superman, their "Man of Steel". He told tall tales that to this day the children would still swear are true. According to John, he had saved a baby bear but had been in a fight with it's mother, and had been shot out of a carnival cannon when the circus came to town. Imagine his parent's disappointment when they returned from the restrooms and realized what they had missed! He also joked that he was the namesake of a very popular pizza chain. John claimed that he had been a stow away on a small boat to Italy when he was just a young boy, and taken under the wing of a famous pizza maker who also happened to be named John. What an imagination he had. He loved to play games—all types of games. Board games, card games, any type of outdoor games. He would just pick up a ball and ask Alex to go outside and play catch. Or go shoot hoops. He helped Caroline make a game called "Shop-opoly" (watch out Monopoly) by drawing the entire game board with her favorite stores and helping create the rules. Things I wouldn't have dreamt of doing. He was a giant kid. Giant but gentle and kind. Approachable. Every child that came into contact with John instantly gravitated toward him. He seemed to be able to make everything funny. Sometimes even the things that weren't.

While this could prove frustrating at times when I was working inside, outside, and upside-downs of a complicated business and also serving as wife and mother, I knew that ultimately it was great for all the kids, so I tried to do everything I was best at, good at, and all the other things that didn't come quite naturally, but had to get done as well.

But John's distraction from the business would lead to tensions and arguments between us. He had too much "Whatever" in him. I may have had too much "Where the heck is it?" in me. But our business played out in a highly competitive arena—construction material supply—during a boom time that was beginning to just show the first faint cracks of what would become the deep economic troubles and - more immediately and importantly to us—the slowing of the greater Phoenix building-and-housing surge.

But as a couple we still rolled together, despite the inevitable stresses that we learned come as the cloudy part of the package when two people work and live together. We had a happy, extremely satisfying family life. A beautiful home. A handful of terrific kids who ensured we were never bored or lonesome. Our social life was centered mostly on school events and charitable causes, and it was satisfying and rewarding. An exciting life inside and outside of the bedroom. Which seemed to be more than I could have ever hoped for. If I was down, John knew just what to say to get me back on my feet. If John was down, I knew to just snuggle up to him for a bit and be silent. It worked every time. It truly was a life that almost anyone would envy. It had its moments of frustrations, but it had mountains of satisfaction. In other words it was a real life, not a forced imitation of one. And who couldn't be happy with that?

However it would be in that one frustrating component of our lives together—the business—where what I assumed were just run-of-the-mill fault lines in our marriage would first appear. The coming doses of reality and unreality that would follow, seeming to arrive as regularly as the Valley Metro, would be more complex and ultimately more devastating than a business off balance.

2.

John was having an affair – possibly several affairs. I knew it. I was absolutely convinced. I had no doubt in my mind. That simple and that lowdown.

I saw signs of it every minute he sat across from me at his desk; I imagined other, more vivid indicators when he was away from the office. There was a John Graves at work and at home, but it was not the John Graves I had married and would swear I knew better than any other man I'd ever known in my life.

He was the man I loved. The man I thought was in love with me. And now I was absolutely sure he was spending his time, our money, his energy on someone or more than one someone he found more deserving. It wasn't exactly the idea of who I was consumed with (though I won't lie: that was no small part of it) but why? Why put a cheap county-fair tattoo on the fine skin of a charmed life? Was there something I hadn't been doing, something that I was doing that I shouldn't have been doing, something I didn't know how to do, something I'd been missing? Was I too demanding? Not demanding enough? Was there some more potent, idealized form of love out there than I could provide for John that he wasn't already receiving from me? I began questioning, wondering if I was to blame for his betrayal.

I would swear in any court—civil, supreme, or even Judge Judy's—that our life together was beautiful – at least up until then. Sure, it wasn't flawless; no true beauty ever is. But for a time it was cool and fun and juicy. Now it seemed that for John, it wasn't enough. Something had changed.

Suspicious behavior gave way to hard proof: money went missing from the business accounts. Not a little bit, and not just once. Enough that it was affecting our ability to do business, and a more than sufficient amount to finance a finely tasteless tawdry affair—even another family.

We were still working at the same location, but I couldn't say we were working together. Still living in the same house, sleeping in the same bed, but they couldn't have felt more like foreign territory if the house had been carried away by a tornado and landed with a thump atop a wicked mistress from the east.

I didn't know what to do, so at first I did what I think every woman who thinks her husband is having an affair did: I tried to deny every bit of evidence I could.If John disagreed with me over some point major or minor, I must have missed some crucial nugget of information he was basing his opinion on. If the bank reported a significant withdrawal from our account, but he couldn't remember making it and wouldn't say where the money went, apparently he was too compassionate or discreet to admit that it went to pay a bill or to help one of our customers out of a tight spot.

Disagreements about the kids schoolwork, recreation, childhood personality conflicts were me being stiff and judgmental, and I needed to chill. If he treated me as if I were invisible, it was because I felt that I had become invisible.

I tried hard to convince myself that everything was OK, even though it wasn't. I told myself that this is a phase, that all couples have their highs and lows. We had just hit an all-time low. I rationalized that perhaps John was feeling overworked, overstressed and underappreciated. So, what did I do? Naturally, as any nurturing woman would do, I tried even harder.

I planned more date nights, I bought more lingerie, and I cooked his favorite meals all in the hopes of bringing back the man who had suddenly checked out.

Those diversions worked for a little while.(Holding your breath in a garage filled with exhaust fumes works for a little while too, as long as you don't try to take another breath.)

Still following the standard jilted-wife playbook, I made the next mandatory move: marriage counseling. The thing about professional paid-for relationship support is that both paying parties have to give a damn for it to work. Here, a typical excerpt for one of our sessions:

Me: "I feel like... I feel like I miss you, even though I'm with you."

John: *Shrug.*

Me: "Can you at least tell me how you feel."**John:** "I feel OK."

Me: "Mmmmm... could you elaborate on that a little."

John: *No response.*

The counselor recommended a psychiatrist, who then prescribed an antidepressant for John.

The emotional lockout, the money disappearing from the bank like the recession had already happened, the complete disconnect between our old lives and this current farce continued long after the pills should have worked their magic, if there was magic to be worked.

There were so many times that out of the blue and without warning and for no reason at all, John would suddenly humiliate and embarrass in public – and also private. We were no longer partners, and this wasn't the man I married. John had checked out. John's public denial that I had anything to do with our business, embarrassments at the kids' school fundraiser, inexplicable, stupefying behavior in front of old friends. Something had to be done. It was time to take the next step.

So, I took it.

It seemed to me, from some reading I'd done and some confidential talks I had with close friends, that there were two ways to go: I could go searching for hard evidence myself. But that seemed like willingly strolling into an emotional minefield wearing nothing but flip-flops and plastic wrap. So I went the other way: I hired a private investigator. It seemed like the right thing to do at the time. I had someone on the case, someone on my side. I could try to salvage our lives, my life, our business, something, anything, without worrying about where John was and what he was doing. I had a professional watcher doing the watching. I was paying her to do the worrying, I'd worry when I had the time; after all, I had a business to run and a family to tend to. But I had a life to continue. I wanted my husband back, though I had no idea where he had gone. I wanted our business back under control. I wanted our home to be our refuge from the world, and not for the world to be a welcome escape from our home.

I was absolutely determined the right result would follow from my actions. Things would straighten out, in time would be better than ever. A poisonous root had infected our family tree, and I meant to have it dug out, chopped into pieces, and burned to ash. John's life with the kids and me could and would be brilliant again, and nothing could convince me otherwise.

One night after a fairly exasperating day at the office, I decided to set up a light, cool, relaxed night of take-out dinner and a movie. John had left work before me, so it would be a nice surprise for him when I showed up carrying the entire evening in my arms. I ordered the food, went to the video store (how dated is that?) to grab a feel-good comedy, and headed home with favorite fare, great entertainment, and in the mood to make things feel right. I pulled into our driveway, stopped in front of the house. The other car that should have been there—with John either about to get out of it or already in the house—wasn't anywhere to be seen.

OK, I told myself, he said he was going to be coming straight home from the office, but things happen. I wasn't thinking catastrophe at this point, just him catching every red light between the office and our home. I was sure he must have been rerouted around construction or caught behind a fender bender. But in the back of my mind, something wasn't right. So I called his cell phone. Surprisingly, he answered right away.

"Um, where are you, John?" I asked, not wanting sound too apprehensive and ruin the evening if there was an easy explanation.
But his answer came back sharp, testy, like who the heck was I to be checking up on him in the first place. "In a parking lot," he said in a strangely surly voice.

"What parking lot would that be, John?" I was trying to keep what still remained of my composure. *Please let this be simple*, I thought. *Let this be less than nothing.*

His answer offered no comfort. "I don't know." He replied without an ounce of emotion.

All right. I tried a slightly different tack. "Do you think you'll be coming home?"

After an agonizing interval he managed to utter a less than reassuring, "Sure." He could say anything he wanted, but I was convinced at that moment that he had found entertainment elsewhere.

Hours later and after several rounds of tears, I had gone to bed, and eventually he did indeed return home.

As I heard John walk into the house, I was thinking that I didn't know much about anything anymore. But one thing I knew was this: Faking sleep is a breeze when you've had plenty of practice faking every waking moment of the day.

Fast forward, if you can, through a life that feels like it's moving against the tide in a sea of wet concrete. Less than a week later I decided to take lunch at home, a break from an overloaded desktop and tension in the office, while John was out in the field checking on the progress of some of our more important projects.

Instead, I found John asleep in the house, slumped in an armchair.

Maybe we'd had the same idea of a restful lunch at home.

I moved to wake him gently. He emerged from his sleep quite slowly. He seemed confused, didn't seem to know exactly where he was or what time it could be, even though the daylight was as bright as only an early Arizona afternoon can be.

He asked me if he had been sleeping, his voice containing all the confusion of a child being awoken at an odd hour and in a strange place.

I asked if he was hungry, and he responded, "OK."

I made us some lunch and we sat together at the table, not talking much. Not talking at all, really. He never touched even a crumb of food.

We went back to work, but I was as baffled as ever, if not more. Was John's behavior that of someone involved in a passionate affair with another woman? And if this was the case, what had I done to deserve this treatment? To me his actions now seemed more like those of someone with a serious drug addiction. That would *at least* provide a rational, if equally unwelcome explanation for some of the money that had gone missing from our business, and for John's suddenly dimmed emotions. But, I told myself, no one could spend as much money as was missing solely on himself—and possibly a few false friends—and survive that kind of a drug addiction. I didn't know enough about any of these scenarios, so I called the counselor we had been seeing to get a more educated slant on just what the heck was going on here. I swear, I was this close to my breaking point. I had no one to depend on, I was in this alone, and with John missing in action, at least for the time being, I had no one else I could completely trust.I decided I would give things a little more time to sort themselves out. I needed to catch my breath, if it could still be caught. I assumed I'd be able to at least luck into a moment when John was lucid and I could work my way to the truth, even if it was a truth I did not want to see or hear.

A couple of days later, I found John at home again in the middle of the afternoon, asleep in the yard. He had taken the dogs out to play. He was oblivious to his whereabouts this day, as he had been when I'd discovered him zonked in the armchair.Forget it. No more fooling around. I took John directly to the counselor with me, and we sat down for a long-overdue serious and absolutely direct discussion. After a brutal and thorough talk with our counselor, the problem—and its solution—finally became obvious: John, our counselor advised, was suffering from a bout of major clinical depression. It wasn't something that was going to be solved by giving him more personal space, decreasing his level of family or work responsibility, or ignoring his symptoms until his emotions stabilized and the problem answered itself. He said he felt that John needed to spend some time in a facility where his behavior could be observed and the best possible combination of therapies could be initiated to effect a long-term cure. If, by chance, there was any kind of an addiction they would surely be the ones to uncover it.

Our counselor suggested Sierra Tucson, a rehabilitation center in the Santa Catalina Mountains just north of the city of Tucson that had an excellent reputation. The therapists at the center were regarded as first rate, and there was no reason to believe that John—who would be scheduled for a month-long program—wouldn't emerge in thirty days a happier, better, more John-like John. It sounded like this offered everything I wanted: my husband and life partner back. But I expected resistance to this idea from John. He hadn't been making good decisions about anything for a long time—not unusual for someone who has clinical depression—and Phoenix, particularly our home and our business, were the limits of his comfort zone, even though he seemingly hadn't felt comfortable at either place for quite some time.

When our counselor made the proposal to us, then asked, "What do you think, John?" I prepared myself for what I thought was the inevitable refusal and subsequent tirade.

John looked benignly at me, at our counselor, and said, "Sounds good." I looked at him as if he was an imposter. I thought to myself, *What have you done with my husband?* Just like that.

Our problems, they assured us, would be solved in a month - swept behind us like crumbs off a kitchen floor, and it came to be with two simple words from the man I loved. They weren't the words "I do," which had made me adore him even more when he had voiced them. But at that moment in our lives, the words "sounds good" were every bit as important as those other two simple syllables had been.

Your Cheatin' Heart

I don't think anyone knows how she would react if she suspected her spouse (or any other term you'd prefer for the person who shares your life) of being emotionally and/or sexually involved with another person. I know that the mere thought of it will simultaneously send your heart and head racing and deaden your soul. Whether it's the first or second thought you have, it's bound to be some variation on this: What is wrong with *me*? How did I push the person I love toward someone else? Any hint of ego you may have had is immediately deflated like a balloon dropping onto a bed of nails. And then, if you don't have definitive proof, you will start to piece together shreds of real and imagined information, which you believe that if you had noticed sooner would have prevented the infidelity from continuing beyond its tentative beginnings, or led you much earlier to the inescapable conclusion that you've been cheated on.

Most of your definitive proof will probably be nonsense, fueled by desperation and depression. It's possible to interpret any private or public act as a sign of infidelity. At the time I started to suspect, then became *convinced*, that John was having an affair, everything he did seemed to confirm my suspicions, pointing only to one inescapable conclusion. When I was trying to parse every small bit of my husband's behavior together, I was also consumed with trying to keep our business moving ahead. I took what was to me the next, logical, practical step—hiring a private investigator—to gather as much unimpeachable proof as possible to support my brokenhearted doubts.

Much later, when events had overtaken my suspicions, and I began to document my experiences, I wondered what signs of infidelity were considered absolute, and what most people did with their suspicions, particularly those who for one reason or another didn't go the same route as I did. I did some of my own research of my own and discovered some common, some bizarre, facts and stats, such as, (1) though men are still more prone to infidelity, women are, unfortunately, catching up fast in the race (different sources claim different percentages of men and women who engage in this activity, but all were in general agreement on how those numbers are trending); (2) Internet cheating, or affairs that begin with Internet contact, is the fastest growing arena for this activity; (3) more cash makes disloyalty more common—simply, money is a magnet that attracts the most attention; and (4) if your spouse is suddenly dressing better or in a different style, is interested in topics you've never heard him or her wax poetically about, and disappears at strange hours, particularly on holidays, you probably have a problem on your hands.

To put it another way, somebody else's hands are probably on your problem.

People who are already an emotional wreck aren't very

good at collecting evidence themselves (trying to check cell phone messages; tracking e-mails, numbers dialed and received, and voice-mails; studying bank statements; and checking the trash for gift receipts, hotels, meals or drink tabs). They lack all objectivity. Eventually, if the truth of the matter (or what they want to believe is the truth) doesn't come to light naturally, they'll employ an investigator. Except for those people determined to cure the problem themselves and keep their relationships alive after the fact. Those people will confront the possibly guilty party with whatever reams or snippets of data they've unearthed.

What comes during and after that kind of conflict is as varied as people are themselves. Be ready for anything. Don't necessarily blindly wish for the best. You probably don't know what the best is. Nobody does.

按按

While I was poking around for information on how other people have handled the specter of infidelity, I happened on an article by a writer named Julie Vincent that introduced me to the concept of "financial infidelity." It provided an interesting and, to me, new angle on the lousy deed, which didn't include a physical, emotional, or sexual component. It seems that money—its lack or misuse—breaks up as many partnerships and marriages as does sexual infidelity. Vincent writes that "it's important to remember that [the faithless person] likely has a form of addiction ... whether it be shopping, gambling, going out to eat constantly, or even simply going through money and not being able to explain where it went." She goes on to say that if the addiction isn't addressed, the financial infidelity won't end.

It became a potent reminder to me that the definition of "fidelity" is not as clearcut as it sounds. And it is almost always likely to be interpreted or misinterpreted solely in the sexual definition. But that's a discussion for another book, another time. Till then I think people in serious relationships would do well to heed the lyrics of a classic Black Crowes song: "Don't give me no lines and keep your hands to yourself."

3.

We planned to head to Sierra Tucson in a week, on a Tuesday morning. The intervening time would give us the opportunity to get the business in order for John's extended absence and my shorter one. We'd have the chance to explain the situation to our families and the kids. And, most importantly, I'd have the time to prepare John for what he was about to face. He had been unusually amenable to the idea of this month-long institutionalization while we were in the counselor's office, but I wasn't convinced he would remain comfortable with the idea as the day of departure came ever closer. Unfortunately, I was right, but not for the relatively simple reasons I had been obsessing over. Our trip to Tucson would turn out not to be an easy one—nor could we wait a week for it to happen.

Within days of our visit to the counselor, John began to go downhill so fast it didn't seem possible. I'd never seen anything like it. He couldn't successfully complete the making of a phone call. Within moments he'd have no idea what he was saying or with whom he was talking. He'd promise to call back in "just a bit", say "something else had come up," then laugh to himself: he had no idea to whom he had just made that promise.I couldn't allow this to continue. I told him, "We're leaving for Sierra today." Now the snappish John began to emerge again, though at first he expressed himself in a relaxed manner.

"I don't want to rush it," he said. "Let's wait until Tuesday." That was three days away, when we were originally scheduled to head south. I wasn't about to wait another hour, much less a few days. But John was insistent.

"We can't go now," he said. "What about the office? Tuesday is plenty soon enough, and that's when I want to go."

I called our counselor. In his opinion John was on a fast track for a complete nervous breakdown and needed to get to Sierra Tucson immediately.

So despite John's strenuous protests we left the next morning. During the drive down, he was curt and irritable. I kept reminding myself that it was not my John being insensitive and unable to focus on anyone but himself. At the time, my stepmother, Jackie was battling breast cancer. (She would battle that awful disease off and on for years before she would inevitably lose her life to it.) She happened to call while we were driving down to Tucson, and John could not or would not hide his annoyance that I was paying attention to someone else, or even talking at all.

I asked if he was particularly troubled with the idea of being away from home for a month. Or if he had any memory of what had been going on for the past six months.

John just shut down and wouldn't respond. Then he opened his eyes as if awakening from a dream and said, "This is a really winding road." Hearing that, I couldn't bring myself to respond as I drove along the ruler-straight highway on the way to Sierra Tucson. I was scared to death.

I'd never seen a treatment center before, and didn't know quite what to expect. Possibilities from a medium-security prison to a new age spa ran through my mind. Fortunately, it was neither. It was a modern, professional setting, welcoming but also not a place that would inspire one to want to linger beyond one's prescribed stay. John and I walked in, and within minutes were confronted with the inevitable ream of paperwork that accompanies any health-facility stay.

I sat with John as he tried to fill out his intake forms. He was writing down outdated, incorrect information; he was unable to spell our children's names. The staff person in charge of intake was kind but clearly troubled by what she was seeing. As John, exhausted from his efforts, took a much-needed break from the pile of papers, the staffer took me aside.

"I'm concerned that your husband's difficulties may be neurological rather than psychological," she said.

I looked at her with a blank expression on my face. I couldn't process what she was saying. For a moment I could imagine what John must have been feeling like as he struggled to fill out the relatively simple but inevitably redundant set of forms.

"Well," I said, "he hasn't been sleeping or eating well for weeks. The last few days he's hardly had anything. I think he's dehydrated." Simple truths simply expressed. I had no idea how desperate I sounded at that moment.

She put her hand on my arm to comfort me and said, "He may not need the kind of help we can offer here."

I pulled away. I didn't want to hear this. "He's having a breakdown. A nervous breakdown. That's what you do here, isn't it?" I knew I was losing it. But the stress of the past months was surfacing here and now, and I didn't feel capable of stopping it. "What do you mean by 'neurological' anyway? What are you saying? We just drove two hours to get here. You have to fix him! I can't take him back home with me!"

Another staff member mercifully steered John away from this angry, surreal confrontation as the intake woman explained that the best course of action would be for the staff to observe John's behavior and monitor his vital signs overnight, then reassess his condition.

By then my breathing, which had become a little labored, was beginning to calm. I said, "He really is dehydrated, you know."

"I know he is," she said, and then continued. "It would be best if you didn't drive back to Phoenix tonight. I think you're exhausted, and you have every right to be." I nodded, relieved that someone was finally understanding what effect this was having on me.

Then she followed with, "We also need you here tomorrow in case we need to move him to a hospital."

The alarm must have been evident on my face.

"We don't know that for sure," she said, trying to reassure me. "We don't know what we'll observe tonight. Just let us take care of your husband and we'll be in touch with you tomorrow."

I was emotionally shot. I was a physical wreck. I walked to John, hugged him goodbye. It was clear he had no idea where he was or what was going on. I didn't want to leave, couldn't bring myself to leave. But when John was led off by a nurse, I was not allowed to follow, and it broke my heart. I couldn't have gotten to the car fast enough. I got inside, slammed the door shut, and called my father in St. Louis, hysterically sobbing. I'm sure he couldn't understand a word through my tears. I was inconsolable. I checked in at the closest hotel I could find, wrought with fear and anxiety.

I couldn't sleep. Who'd be able to? This time I called my mother and told her how the staff at Sierra was implying that John's problem was neurological, but they didn't go beyond using that single word. "Do you think it could be something like early onset Alzheimer's," I asked, not really expecting an answer.

My mother did her best to put my mind at ease. "You have to trust that they're doing the right thing," she said. "They're going to do their best for John. You're going to know much more in the morning. But in the meantime, you've got to get some rest. You have to have a clear mind for tomorrow. For your sake and John's."

I heard my mother's advice, but I wasn't able to follow it.

"I'm going to call over there right now. I just need to know that he's all right."

I dialed the number and got the nurse on duty.

John wasn't all right: he'd had a few small seizures since after arriving there.

"No one called me," I said, trying to sound composed. "I'm coming back over right now."

The nurse told me not to do that. They were monitoring him, and he was safe.

"What are you monitoring him *for*?" I asked.

"I really don't know," she said, with more honesty but far less detail than I needed.

I repeated my mantra of "He's dehydrated" for the hundredth time, and the nurse responded that John was on IV fluids and they'd be watching him closely through the night. I knew she meant this to be comforting, but I was at the point where I couldn't imagine any good coming of anything. I knew you could as easily watch someone die in the night as watch him rest comfortably in bed.

The next morning arrived, and no one had called me. So I called, left a message, and when the doctor arrived, they called back, informing me that John was being transported to the emergency room at Northwest Oro Valley Community Hospital. They were going to do a CAT scan and wanted me there. I was still in some sort of denial; I insisted on continuing to believe John was simply suffering from a nervous breakdown. I couldn't understand what a high-tech X-ray could determine about such a condition.

When I arrived at the hospital John—strangely enough—was sitting in the lobby, waiting for his turn on the scanner. I sat next to him and looked him in the eyes. Something was not quite right there: he was looking at me like he knew me, but he wasn't sure how or from where. I touched his face, brushed back his hair a little. But he seemed afraid of me. I began to remind him who I was, who he was, but he stopped me with a wave of his fingers.

"Shh," he said, "would you please stop talking."

As I sat there, trying not to fall apart, a hospital attendant arrived with a gurney, asked John to scoot up on it, and wheeled him off to his test.

I think I sat there blinking for ten minutes, as if I were looking directly into the sun.

After a short while I was led to a small room, where John already sat, placid and utterly unaware of the potential ramifications of what we were about to hear. I knew I might have been overdramatizing the moment in my head, but I felt like we were waiting for a verdict on a capital crime.

Dr. Catherine Sander, who had read the results of the CAT scan came into the room, and was as straight and candid with us as any doctor ever had been and ever would be.

"You must realize by now that John's problem isn't a nervous breakdown," she began.Well, no, I hadn't, but I nodded my head anyway.And then she said, "John has a tumor that's creating a large amount of pressure on his brain.I asked, "What do we do to find out if it's benign or malignant?"

She reluctantly replied, "It is cancerous. Treatments can extend his life, but his condition is terminal."

The man I loved had just been handed a death sentence.

Glioma

It is a word ugly enough to make you wish your mouth and tongue couldn't make the motions necessary to say it. Glioma. Or more exactly, and more to the point, *Glioblastoma multiforme*. On a list of things you would ban from this world, brain tumors—particularly this type of sinister, aggressive, cancerous growth—would have to be near the top of the list, even if you are the ultimate misanthrope; even if you hate dogs (which are also strangely susceptible to this particularly horrible disease).

These devastating brain tumors are relatively rare (fewer than twenty thousand are diagnosed annually in the United States), unpredictable (there are no blood tests, no genetic test nor marker that can predict who will develop glioma; there appears to be no hereditary component to it either), and always incurable (though different treatment regimens can extend the life of a patient, the commutation of that grim sentence generally lasts no more than ten to sixteen months).

The warning signs of glioma mirror so many other physical and psychological disorders that a tumor—and this particular tumor— is one of the last things anyone would blame this type of behavior on. Symptoms include headaches, confusion, seizures, nausea, arm and/or leg numbness, and personality changes. But, as was the case with John, he never talked about any "symptoms" as such; he complained that his eyes hurt one time and never mentioned it again. The confusion and personality changes, I took as "symptoms" of something very different, as did behavioral specialists. Another significant problem with diagnosing gliomas is that they frequently produce no symptoms until they get to a relatively huge size.

Glioblastomas rise up from the brain tissue itself, from the cells that support the nerve cells, and steadily, inexorably kill the brain tissue it displaces. There is no stopping it, though its progress can be slowed somewhat if it's discovered early enough in a young patient (under forty) and with very aggressive treatment—surgical removal of at least 98 percent of the tumor, followed by radiation, chemotherapy, and steroid therapy. And even with that massive hard-line assault against the cancer, the average survival time of a glioma patient is about eleven months. Those deciding to forgo, or not knowing enough to seek out, treatment generally survive three months from the time the first tumor begins to form.

All in all, you'd rather have almost anything else other than glioma. You'd rather have a dead-shot hired killer trying to track you down. At least then you'd know what you were fighting, and you might have a chance to get the first shot off.

Glioma is indiscriminate, of course, as is most disease (though, indeed, poverty and environmental factors can make certain diseases more likely to strike a particular population). But among the well-known figures that glioma has victimized, according to Greg Brian's "Famous Deaths Caused by Glioblastoma and Other Brain Tumors," include George Gershwin, who survived but one month after being diagnosed (he first began complaining of intense headaches a year before, while he was writing *Porgy and Bess*); film critic Gene Siskel, actress Irene Ryan (Granny on *The Beverly Hillbillies*, she was performing on Broadway in "Pippin" when she collapsed onstage and died two weeks later); Mary Shelley, author of *Frankenstein* and one of the first notable individuals to die from a confirmed brain tumor; French film director Francois Truffaut; O.J. Simpson defense attorney Johnnie Cochran; Lee Atwater, chairman of the Republican Party; and, most recently, Senator Ted Kennedy.

Senator Kennedy and his family reportedly decided on the most aggressive treatment regimen now possible—surgery, chemotherapy (usually a medication called temozolomide), radiation, steroids— and still survived only fifteen months after being diagnosed.

I knew none of this at the moment we heard John's diagnosis. I would come to this information, and learn the progressively overwhelming practical demands of coping with this disease, as time and opportunity afforded, and through hard experience.

I knew none of this at the moment we heard John's diagnosis. I would come to this information, and learn the progressively overwhelming practical demands of coping with this disease, as time and opportunity afforded, and through hard experience.

4.

An understatement, really the only one, from Dr. Sander, the finest medical professional John and I dealt with, with his terrible diagnosis. After telling us (in truth, me, since John had laid back down and fallen asleep) the grim treatment options for glioma, she told me that John could well survive for a year if we did everything, but the patient "isn't the same person they were before." She continued on to say, "Treatment is optional."

In most instances you hear those three words in reference to a minor injury or illness that will heal itself in a relatively short while. This, not one of those times. I was taking it very hard. Any composure I had been maintaining had fallen away.The rest is pretty much a blur. I know that I made several phone calls, received a lot of varying opinions, and spoke with Dr. Sanders several times. I was doing the best I could to cope, but I wasn't in a coping mode. I was, in fact, inconsolable.

John had updated his living will when we were married and had specified that he did not want life-extending measures taken in case of an illness or injury that would clearly be terminal. But this was more a slow-motion crisis than one would usually think of for that circumstance, a crawl rather than a headlong charge through the valley of death. The interpretation was mine to make and required a crystal-clear mind, but at this moment I couldn't be sure exactly what my obligation was.

Dr. Sanders offered the option of treating John with steroids, which would reduce the swelling in his brain and would keep him alive and comfortable for a few days.

Only a few days.

Surgery. I wanted John to have the surgery. I couldn't choose a couple of semi-conscious days of meaningless life that the simple course of steroids would offer. To me, that would truly violate the spirit of the living will John had created. Surgery was hope. Surgery was time. Meaningful time with his family, to give him time to reflect on his life.

If time seemed as if it were standing still before I made that decision, it went into hyperdrive the moment I settled on a course of action. We would be helicoptered to the Barrow Neurological Institute of St. Joseph's Hospital in Phoenix, where John would have surgery to remove as much of the tumor as possible without destroying the surrounding brain tissue.

I planned not to leave as much as a dime's width of distance between John and me during the flight. I wanted to hold onto him as if his life depended on it, as if I could transfer some of my life into him as we flew over the baking landscape below. Just as I finished readying myself for the flight, a hospital staffer approached me and said, "Sorry. You can't go with your husband, because adding one more person will exceed the weight limit." So, I offered to strip down to the bare essentials in the dead of winter, just so that I could accompany my husband to the hospital in Phoenix. The answer was still no.

So I collapsed as I watched the helicopter lift off.

My children, Alex and Caroline, were John's youngest "kids." He had three children from his first marriage, and had adopted the son of his second wife. Alex and Caroline's father lives in Phoenix and has always been a big part of their lives. But John was, as they called him, their "Big Daddy." They lived with him for the longest period of their lives, and through the last act of his life, before his illness began, during the phase when the cancer began to markedly change his behavior, and then through his traumatic illness and death.

They were present, eyewitnesses and earwitnesses to all the episodes of John's and my life that I write about in "Checking Out." Your kids are the most significant reason to never walk away from the trials and tribulations of your life. Not to every action, of course, but they saw enough—too much for people so young—of John's and my experiences, and the results and emotional aftermaths, I think, to have important insights into this difficult situation.

They had their own intense stresses as a result of what was hap-pening to our family. But people are sometimes so focused on their own pain and responsibilities, the kids can get overlooked. Or their opinions aren't deemed worthy of exploration.

I never felt that way about Alex and Caroline. We laughed and cried, worked and fought together. I know they had feelings that crossed over into hateful territory toward me because of some of my grief-induced poor choices and illogical actions. I wanted them to have a forum to express their point of view on the story I told in this book, But I didn't know how open they would be to a face-to-face interview with me.

I asked if they'd be willing to answer some questions about what they saw and heard and felt during that time. That I'd make a list, word the queries in a way that wouldn't lead them to one answer or another. And like the great kids they are, they both agreed.

I was surprised how quickly they came back with their answers. Maybe it was something of a catharsis for them to be able to ad-dress these issues in a way that didn't put pressure on them when they answered. I think their answers to the tough questions I asked them are absolutely honest and courageous, absolutely fearless and without guile.

These are their own words. Throughout the book are Alex and Caroline's personal accounts.

ॐ✄

Alex: *I found out John was sick when I was at my friend Clay's house. His mom's friend Gretchen called me outside and told me that my mom wanted to talk to me. I got on the phone. I could hear her bawling, and I immediately knew for some reason that it was a brain tumor. A lot of things had been happening at home before John was diagnosed, but I never believed that it was because of a brain tumor, or even him being sick. I thought that my mom and John were just fighting the way some people do. I just assumed they were going to be getting a divorce. There were really only a couple times that John seemed to be really strange. Not his normal self at all. Once, he forgot to pick me up from practice at my school. I called him and he had completely forgotten, which was not like him at all. I asked him where he was, and he said, "I don't know." John always knew what he was doing.*

Caroline: *I found out about John when I was at my best friend Taylor's house. I was in her room with her and my mom called. I asked her what was up and she was crying. I don't remember exactly what she said but it was along the lines of, "John has a brain tumor." I immediately fell on the bed and just started crying and hyperventilating. Taylor asked me what was wrong, so she started to cry too. I was completely unaware there was anything wrong with him at all. But after I found out the kind of tumor he had and how it affects people, I started to remember a few things that weren't really like John. For instance, not knowing where he was sometimes, not having the "right" emotional response to some things, and the arguments he and my mom had been having.*

Alex: *I did not know what to think after I found out more about the tumor. I was in complete shock. I didn't want to believe, but I knew it was absolutely true. It all made sense. One thing I didn't realize is it was an absolute death sentence. I thought he could be cured, and I didn't find out for a while that he couldn't be. That crushed me. I didn't want to understand it. I just didn't want it to be true.*

Caroline: *I remember John and my mom going to Tucson suddenly, supposedly for work. My mom's friend Janet picked me up from school. I was really mad that Janet, and not my mom, had come to get me for some reason. I told my mom I didn't want Janet in the house so I could be alone. But my Mom insisted that she stay, so she stayed outside on the patio and I was in my room. I really just needed to be alone.I was confused and upset. I didn't know why she had to be there. I yelled at my mom over the phone. But later she called and said that John was getting flown somewhere because he got sick on the way to Tucson. I asked Janet to drive me to Taylor's house, and that's where I found out what happened.*

Alex: *When I got the news, I was hanging out with my friends Clay, Kevin, and Will. I stayed outside for a while because I was a mess and didn't want my friends to see me like that. Gretchen asked me if I wanted Clay's sister to go in and tell my friends what was going on. I said absolutely not. I didn't want anyone to know. But I realized they'd find out eventually, and it would be better to let them know now, because they were best friends.*

It took me hours to go back inside. I just stood at the door because I felt I was going to break down. Then I sat down and just started to cry. Clay and Kevin walked over and patted me on the back, then walked outside. Will sat in front of me and said the nicest thing anyone said to me through all the tough times with John. I remember it word for word. He said, "I'm sorry, man. I am here for you if you need anything. We're all here for you."

Caroline: *I told my best friend, Melissa, right away, but that was it. I went to my friend Casey and Andrew's birthday party at Andrew's house; my mom's best friend, Lori, took me there. I saw all my girlfriends standing in a circle, and I walked up to them and said, "He has a tumor," and just broke down. But the party was at least a distraction. It took my mind off things, and I didn't know until afterwards just how bad things were.*

At my school chapel the next day, the priest asked everyone to pray for John and Mom and Alex and me. Nothing could be a secret anymore.

There was no way I could drive myself back to Phoenix. I wouldn't have made it out of the parking lot without requiring the attention of the emergency room myself. The hospital staff realized that as well and ordered a car service to take me back to Phoenix. The desert I'd just driven through the day before and had planned to fly over just minutes ago seemed utterly unfamiliar as I trailed far behind and below the man whose life I so wanted to preserve.

Arriving in Phoenix less than two hours later, I was driven directly to Barrows. I wasn't sure exactly what to expect, but what I saw was chaos and stress. I can't even remember anymore (I think I've completely suppressed it) who was there and who wasn't. But everyone was desperate for answers and encouragement, and I just didn't have much of either to give. When Alex and Caroline finally did arrive, all I could do was rush to them and hold them to me as tightly as I could, as tightly as I'd wanted to hold John on his flight from Tucson.

An endless wait, and a cascade of questions I couldn't begin to answer: details about the surgery (which wasn't close to taking place yet), the cancer, the tumor itself. Questions I can answer now by rote, I couldn't begin to imagine the correct answers to then. I just wanted to hold my kids and see my husband. It was a lifetime before I finally got the OK to go down to see John.

He was in a private room, thank God. I couldn't have stood to have to make small talk with another patient or their equally freaked-out visitors, nor they with me, I imagined, if that had been the case. John looked peaceful, eyes closed, but I wasn't sure if he was asleep or not. I placed my hand on his as carefully as I would have on a newborn's head.

He smiled at me. He opened up his eyes. People talk about million-dollar smiles when they refer to actors and models. Uh-uh. Not even close. This was a million-dollar smile you'd pay a hundred times that for if you were asked. I wasn't even sure he had any idea who I was. But the man I loved was alive, and the look on his face said he was happy to be here and with my being here with him. That was more than good enough for me at the moment.

Enter, then, another doctor. Buzzkill. "We want to do another scan," he said matter-of-factly. "I've been looking over Mr. Graves's records."

"A scan for what?" I asked. I'd seen the results of the CAT scan in Tucson. The image was indelibly etched in my mind and, according to the medical team there, its nature was unmistakable.

"We're not sure what we're dealing with here," he said. "This could just be an infection. And that would obviously be treated in a completely different way."

Was he saying it might not be cancer at all? Just an infection of some kind? Was a brain infection better or worse than a brain tumor?

"How do you get an infection in your brain?" I asked. I guess I knew it was possible to get an infection just about anywhere, but to me the brain was the least exposed, and therefore the least likely, part of the body to get infected with anything.

"Look, we don't know what exactly is going on here. And we want to be absolutely sure, don't we?"

Well, heck yes, we did. But I was sure, or at least I thought I was, in Tucson. Now we were stepping back on the spinning wheel of misfortune.

John was whisked away to have an MRI. I went back to the lobby to face the fusillade of questions that would be coming at me hard and fast. After being unable to offer virtually any solace in the way of information to anyone, I was— thankfully, I suppose—called back to John's room by a Barrows doctor after the scan was complete.I sat down, ready to hear anything: it had all been a mistake, it was worse than we'd imagined, it was better than we'd hoped.

"The original diagnosis was accurate," he said. "Your husband has a *glioblastoma multiforme* in the left frontal lobe."

It was then that I received a lesson in anatomy and brain function that I never wanted to learn. The frontal lobe is the last part of the brain to reach what can best be described as maturity. If it gets damaged by accident or disease or, as in John's case, a large, fast-growing malignant tumor, spontaneity and flexibility of thought breaks down; the logical process of understanding risks and rules is diminished; social, sexual, and creative abilities and impulses can fade or increase; people become easily distracted, may start to talk a lot more—or a lot less; and they can lose the linked senses of smell and taste.

And so taken as a whole, or piece by piece, how in the world is someone not schooled in the ways of brain function (me, in this specific instance) supposed to put all that together and come to the conclusion that someone—say a husband or wife—has a massive brain tumor? The symptoms don't show up at the same time, and may not display themselves to you at all. How do you know that the person you love just hasn't lost interest in you and your life together? I didn't. I honestly couldn't have. The symptoms are a jigsaw puzzle with half the pieces missing and the other half only visible when you're not looking. But hearing it all laid out here now, what had been happening over the past several months suddenly seemed clear as a perfect pane of glass.

Considering John's symptoms, the doctors guessed—it's really not possible to be sure with glioma—that the tumor had begun to develop less than a year before. But exactly how long, no one could know. Even if the surgical team removed as much of it as their fine skills would allow, it was certain to grow back as aggressively as ever. It just isn't possible to remove every cancerous cell of a glioma, and chemo and radiation can't blast or poison every enemy cell.

These are not facts and decisions you want to digest quickly. But that's the only choice you have, because glioma works on its own time schedule, not at your convenience.

I said, almost as if talking to myself, "Maybe surgery isn't the best thing for John."

I was shaken out of my daze by the surgeon, who related a story of his father's experience as a glioma patient. He'd had the surgery and had lived a fine year afterward. Had even kept playing golf.

I didn't want to hear it. Not at that moment. All I could think was that my young, handsome, vital husband is not your father. This was my husband, my contemporary, my life-loving companion. We were raising a family together. This was not a man who had the luxury of having lived a long full life and was now in the comfortable position of being able to watch the world spin from a grandparent's distance. It was an instant reaction that I did not put into words. It wasn't consciously mean-spirited, and it was never meant to be. I know that it sounds harsh, but the world and the choices it was offering me at the moment seemed so much more than just harsh.

I needed John. And not just for a year but for the rest of a long, long lifetime together. Yes, I understood the two men had a common diagnosis, but any similarity ended right there. I couldn't make the leap of equivalence.The only response I could muster to the surgeon was to grasp onto the one concrete example of the good life given. "We don't play golf," I said.

The surgeon didn't respond. I don't know if I'd sounded confused or hostile or had even answered in English. (I still have a sense of deep-seated anxiety about my reaction at that moment.) He only repeated that there was no reason to believe that John couldn't have a very good year.

Again, bouncing around in my head was the question, "A very good year as defined how?"

I was left alone to try to characterize that myself.

I looked at John, at the calendar on the wall. It was Tuesday, the day we were originally scheduled to arrive at Sierra Tucson for John's treatment for the now obviously nonexistent nervous breakdown. I suddenly realized that if no other obvious symptoms had occurred while I was with John and we had waited till Tuesday for our drive to Tucson, John would be finished by now. His true condition would only have been diagnosed during an autopsy.

I knew then I owed him the possibility of that year. It was a decision he may have resented, considering the terms of his living will. But I wanted him to have a chance at that "golfing year" whether we golfed or not.I said yes to the surgery, and then I went home.

Alex: *John and my mom fought constantly and very angrily. I never saw my mom and real dad fight. I never heard them fight. I had never seen or heard John or my mom fight either. But then it started up out of nowhere.I don't know why, but I always stick up for the underdog or the "other" side of the story when someone is winning a fight. And in this case when my mom would talk or complain to me about John, I would stick up for him. I'd tell her she was over-reacting and to stop. I didn't want to hear it. But, they really didn't confide in me. Even if they had tried, I would have shut them down because I didn't want to know what was going on.*

Caroline: *John and my mom had been arguing a lot. Their bedroom door was slammed shut and locked, and then there was just* *screaming. I felt bad for John because my mom was just yelling and yelling and he kind of just accepted it. He never defended himself, which was kind of his attitude all of the time. He let things flow and didn't want to disappoint anyone or start any drama.*

5.

Though it may seem an impossible stretch of the imagination for some people, there is such a thing as too much lasagna.

I arrived home alone from the hospital feeling rack-stretched and played out. I was moving on pure autopilot: left foot goes here, right foot goes straight and slightly ahead of the left. I made it to the kitchen. Something was different here. Things were not as I'd left them. This was my kitchen, right? I looked around a kitchen full of food. Fresh food, and in superabundance. The beautiful truth was breaking through: an angel, or angels, unknown had filled the shelves with necessities and small luxuries. An impure thought then, writ in neon, illuminated my mind: holy shit. I couldn't help but smile and finally relax a little at the thought of the people who had delivered this kindness, and would somehow continue to during John's stay in the hospital and long after.Word spread quickly, and everyone seemed to step to the plate to help out. The parents of Alex and Caroline's schoolmates coordinated efforts like a suburban culinary drill team and delivered dinner to the house every night for a year. There always seemed to be lasagna, created in nearly every imaginable permutation, in the freezer and the fridge. I don't remember ever encountering one made of fruit, but that may just be a willful memory lapse on my part. It was a remarkable thing, the purest kind of love people are capable of. But after the events of the coming year were over and gone, neither the kids nor I ever desired another close encounter of the lasagna kind. That pasta-logical block is true to this day. (Thank you, though, dear friends, and apologies to Italy and Italian chefs everywhere.)

These same people also supplied me with the latest research and possible referrals for John's condition. To be the center of a new, ultra-focused community dedicated to getting you through calamity is humbling in the best sense. It offers a rare vacation from your ego, affording the mixed blessing of absolute freedom to concentrate on the hard, complicated circumstances at hand.

John had begun to receive steroid therapy as soon as he had returned to Phoenix and been admitted to Barrows. Surgery, no matter how essential, was out of the question until the swelling in his brain subsided. The steroids had good, but still troubling, effects. John was in good spirits and consistently knew who I was, though that wasn't the case with everyone who came to see him. We spoke quite a bit, though his side of the conversation didn't always quite mesh with what I was talking about. But still, it was hope, still handsome, tall, and able to share a smile and I felt lucky to have that.

When my son, Alex, came to the hospital for a visit, he was greeted by John with an enthusiastic, "Hey, man!" Alex loved it, felt that beautiful naïve sense of hope one gets from the faintest hint of light. If it gave my son encouragement, who was I to complain? But I soon realized that anyone who walked into the room received that same enthusiastic greeting. John had happened upon a welcome that worked to please just about anyone. I can't say if it was a conscious choice or just a reflex he'd developed, but in the end, I knew it wasn't much of a sign of genuine healing. His answers to the questions the staff would ask time and time again varied with each inquiry. Everyday, and possibly every few hours, the staff would ask John if he knew where he was and why he was there. Every time was a different answer. One time he said he was there for eye surgery, another time because he had been in a car accident, and that's the way it went; every time a different answer. Sometimes he just wouldn't answer their simple questions at all. But his ability to communicate even on the basic level meant the swelling had abated, and that would make his life-extending surgery possible.

The day before the scheduled procedure, my mother had flown in from St. Louis for support. I received a call from one of the nurses urging me to come down immediately, that John had thrown off his hospital gown, was attempting to pull the IV line out of his arm, and was insisting that it was time to go home. So we drove like bandits to the hospital and valet parked. As I was racing to get to the elevator to save my husband from anymore humiliation, my mother took a quick detour to the Starbucks line in the hospital lobby. Stunned, I didn't have time to explain to her that coffee wasn't my first priority at this moment. So, I told her to meet in his room and I raced to the elevator. When I walked into the room, there sat John, dressed in his Sunday-best birthday suit anticipating my arrival to take him home. He saw me and said, "I really want to go home now."

"And that's where we want you too," I said, "but you need to be here for a bit. All right?"

There was a frozen moment. I wasn't sure what was going to happen. He stopped pulling at the IV and I helped him back into his gown. It was as simple as that. I reminded that he would be having surgery the next day and needed to get some sleep. So I spent some restful time with him, and when I left he seemed like any other patient, waiting for some unknown procedure or other to be performed. Small favors, you learn to love them.

I walked out to the parking garage, more exhausted from the encounter than I really should have been. I sat in my car, just collecting my thoughts in the deep concrete shade. I closed my eyes for a minute, trying to shut out all input for a few moments. Naturally, my cell phone rang, because that's what they're programmed to do. They know some-how the last moment you want them to ring, then sudden-ly there's that darn ringtone you thought was so adorable when you downloaded it.

Don't answer it, I thought. Give yourself a break, just this once.

I pressed the answer key. The weakness and the worry.It was the private investigator I had hired seven and a half lifetimes ago to discover with whom John was having an extramarital affair.

I had literally forgotten completely about her."Okay, so far …" she began. "Wait," I said, cutting her off. "Let me tell you what's been going on. I'm pretty sure you've never heard this before." And I filled her in on what had transpired since she had started her investigation: that my husband had just been diagnosed with brain cancer, and that all of my suspicions about him having an affair or even several affairs had been debunked. When I finished my monologue, there was a sort of stunned silence on the other end of the phone. Then she said, "Wow, this is definitely a first. I don't know what else to say."

I promised myself to feel guilty about my suspicions later. I needed to rest in anticipation of what was coming next. Surgery Day. Doctors, nurses, trying to prepare me for all imaginable eventualities. But one thing no one can prepare you for—and this may sound petty, but I ask you please don't judge until you've confronted this yourself— is the first time you see the incision site from a neurosurgical procedure. It is not subtle; it is a war wound. How do you deconstruct someone's skull and expect something good to come from it? I know firsthand that it can and does happen. But you will never believe it unless you, God forbid, actually see it or experience it.

As John began to emerge from the anesthesia, the staff immediately started to ask him questions, trying to establish how he'd come through the operation.

A day or so later, they asked him questions such as: "Do you know why you're here?"

He didn't. It's not that John wouldn't provide an answer, but that answer was never the same as one he'd already given. He was asked to identify colors, try his hand at simple puzzles. His success rate wasn't great, but it wasn't hopeless either. John also seemed to lack any enthusiasm for any of the challenges with which he was being presented.

But he did begin to improve slowly, hour by hour, with "improvement" having a very limited definition.

I spent a lot of time with him in his room. It was the most lucid that he would ever be again. We acknowledged Valentine's Day and he asked me to snuggle up with him on his hospital bed, so that we could celebrate it together by watching his favorite new program, Deal or No Deal. I have fond memories of that day, watching him drift off to sleep as I quietly snuck out of the room and headed home.

His physical strength came back surprisingly quickly, though, and the day for him to leave the hospital came upon us suddenly. To my surprise my husband, who had been rushed by helicopter from Tucson at the edge of death less than a week before, walked—no wheelchair in sight—out of the hospital and into the passenger seat of my car. He had been in the hospital a total of six days. John reacted to my nervousness of watching him nonchalantly walk out of the hospital by patting my arm and saying, "It's fine. It's not like I just had brain surgery or anything." A sure sign that my husband was with me.

I wanted to laugh, looked to his face to make sure he was making a conscious joke. It was obvious he wasn't. He couldn't understand why he would need a wheelchair to get to the car, something he'd done hundreds of times in his life.

So, yes, he did it, like an ordinary man under ordinary circumstances. And after two weeks of literally having his head examined, I drove him along roads that might possibly have seemed familiar to him, not to the land of anxiety and lasagna, but just home. Our home.

Life at the Top—Neurosurgery

Dr. Frank Vertosick Jr. wrote a remarkable book called When the Air Hits Your Brain. The title comes from a neurosurgeon's list of axioms about the dramatic, often unpredictable, behavioral changes in a person who has had surgery on their brain. (In this case, the title is culled from Rule #1—"You ain't never the same once the air hits your brain." Numbers 2 and 3? "The only minor operation is one that someone else is doing, and if the patient isn't dead, you can always make him worse if you try hard enough.")

Neurosurgery is the most difficult, time-consuming, and stressful of medical specialties. One slight incorrect movement or judgment can leave your patient irreparably damaged or dead. Workdays are often twenty hours—or longer. In reading dozens of Web postings by neurosurgeons and their family members, the family lives of many neurosurgeons are either nonexistent or hold a distant second place to a surgeons career. One must be somewhat obsessive to be a dedicated, effective neurosurgeon, and the toll it takes on the personal lives of these remarkably talented men and women is significant.

So why would a person take on such a daunting task? Perhaps it is the immense challenges and satisfaction at being able to accomplish remarkable, skillful results in people who are likely to either die or have their lives profoundly compromised if no one steps up to face those tests. And the personal achievement of having an intimate knowledge of the most complex and isolated organ in the human body.

Reading a bit about the structure of the brain, one learns that certain areas of the brain are more "forgiving" than others to surgical invasion, but the frontal lobes are an interesting case of structures that are incredibly delicate, yet able to compensate—to a degree—if there is damage to only one of the pair. That ability to compensate also allows a patient's symptoms to be somewhat invisible to the patient himself (as was the case with John Graves), and inexplicable to those around him. This description from Another Day in the Frontal Lobe by Katrina Firlik offers a remarkable window on what happens to someone with compromised frontal lobes, which is exactly what was occurring inside John's head as his tumor developed:

"The large frontal lobes, in particular, can be quite forgiving, especially when only one side is involved. It's not unusual to see a frontal lobe tumor, for example, grow to impressive citrus fruit proportions before the patient even detects a problem. In fact, the patient often does not detect a problem at all. It is frequently a spouse or friend who insists on the doctor appointment, explaining: 'He's just not right, but I don't know what it is.'

"The frontal lobes harbor quite sophisticated functions... They make up the largest section of the brain and are the most recently evolved. We can thank, or blame, our frontal lobes for much of what we consider to be our personality and intelligence. Damage to the frontal lobes can be subtle, including changes in insight, mood, and higher-level judgment (the 'executive functions')... There is a redundancy and resilience to certain brain functions. What is compromised in one portion can sometimes be compensated for in another. Even if the brain doesn't compensate directly, the patient often can cope indirectly, without even realizing it. If a person develops minor difficulty with memory, for example, he may start to write more things down, thereby maintaining the otherwise seamless flow of his existence."John's surgery involved removal of a large tumor from the frontal lobe, as well as removal of some undamaged brain tissue (what would have been referred to as a lobotomy if it had been performed for psychological illness rather than removal of a malignant mass). So this surgery, even when highly successful, can bring with it significant side effects, including depression, memory loss, battles with balance, coordination, speech, vision, abusive and violent behavior, and impaired muscle function. Some patients also experience inordinate (but quite understandable) fear at the slightest pain or dizziness that occurs after surgery.In short, damage from a tumor or from surgery to the frontal lobe will result in significant alterations in movement, intelligence, reasoning, behavior, memory, personality, planning, decision-making, judgment, initiative, inhibition, and mood. In essence, everything that makes a person "human."

John had indeed been able to walk out of the hospital, into my car, and into our house. But those would literally be baby steps in the uncharted journey of the coming months, which would, by turns, be satisfying and frustrating, tender and terrifying.Our lives hung by the thinnest thread of spider-spun silk. John's future was, to a tragic degree, a future foretold. Mine, though, seemed completely hidden from view, though it would ultimately be shaped by every choice, right and wrong, I would make as I fought to keep my husband safe, alive, and as content as his illness would allow.

6.

John talked. John talked like John. About what had happened to him. About what was going on in the house. About the kids and their schoolwork and their sports. He talked to my brother over the phone. He expressed real desires to accomplish things in the future. Not fantastic things, but things grounded in reality and possibility.

We were waiting for John's surgery and new state of mind to stabilize enough to begin his chemo and radiation therapies. And during this time, John seemed very much himself. Not all the time by any means, but better than he had been in months. It gave me hope, maybe too much hope, but at that time I was happy to accept too much over none at all.

Some of the things we spoke of during this period of lucidity were mournful things: cremation and where the ashes should be placed (some in his Iowa hometown, some to remain in Phoenix, where his children would grow to adulthood). He told me that he did indeed want the chemo and radiation. I felt if not vindicated, at least more at ease with the decisions I had already made.

This was a peaceful time, and it made me long for a future with John that stretched past the horizon. But I also needed to keep reminding myself that this was a temporary state. What would come during and after the intense therapies John was about to go through was entirely unpredictable. So I kept these days like gold coins.

At John's two-week follow-up visit I told the oncologist of the conversations we'd been having, of John's genuinely peaceful nature, and what he dreamed of for the future of the kids, and for us. He was still able to dream of those things, and he expressed them beautifully, but not with complete understanding of the impossibility of those desires.

The oncologist, though, seemed to take this information with what I felt was too much optimism, and it made me uneasy. I thought a physician who'd probably dealt with a hundred other patients like John would understand that his confidence was based more in steroids than in reality. I was wrong.

She asked, "Have you been back to work, John?"

I didn't say anything. I can't quite imagine the look that must have been on my face, but at that moment I kept my thoughts to myself. Back to work? How could she not know that that was an impossibility?

She said she felt it was time to go ahead with the chemo and radiation. As she put it, "We might be surprised at how much and the quality of time they'll get you."

Maybe it was because she wasn't seeing him at home, where he really couldn't do much of anything on his own. Or perhaps it was a positive frame of mind oncologists have to develop to deal with such dire circumstances day in and day out. She was imagining far greater things than what were happening at home, and taking every small sign as something bigger than it actually was.

"We're going to start with the chemotherapy," she continued. "There's an excellent chance that will earn us a good number of months here."

For the first time during the appointment, John shifted in his chair, moving forward slightly toward the doctor. He had a look of ...I don't know how to describe it exactly. Disbelief? Apprehension? Ignorance?

He turned to me and asked, "Am I going to die?"

Before I could answer, the doctor intruded. "Not just yet. We're talking about your treatment to put that day off as long as possible."

I looked at his face, muting the volume on the too-cheery cancer doctor. Even though we'd talked at length about plans for his memorial and his earthly remains, it was clear to me now that he hadn't really understood the true nature of those talks. That his future had an expiration date and it was going to arrive sooner than he had anticipated.

I let the doctor go on till she was finished. There was no point in stopping her here or there to question some point. John wasn't going to understand the ramifications of any answers, and I knew what we were facing.

We left the office. The meeting had left me feeling that either the world I was living in was surreal or the rest of the world was. But it had to be one or the other. As we sat in the car quietly for a few moments, John turned to me and said, "I didn't know I was going to die. Did you?"

I nodded my head. "I thought you understood that," I said.

This conversation was breaking my heart.

But John simply looked out the window of the car, no emotion showing on his face.

"I'm worried about you," he said. "I'll be fine out there. But you're going to be all by yourself."

I was crying. I simply nodded my head in understanding.

Caroline: When John came home [from Barrows, after his operation], we spent a lot of time together. We watched a lot of The Price is Right. We played games, simple ones that I knew he would un-

derstand. It was hard for me to pick out games to play. He wanted to play certain ones, but I just knew he would have a really hard time with most of them. Most of the time, we would be playing a game and I could tell he would be getting frustrated and embarrassed because it was stressing or confusing him, and he would want to stop. But, he was John! He didn't give up! So he tried to hang in there, and I just felt so bad for him because I knew he really wanted to stop, But I didn't know what to do or say.

I tried to spend as much time with him as I could. I liked spending time with him! Once, when he was already sick, I was in my room and he came by, poked his head in, and I said, "Yes?" and he said, "Just coming to say "I love you!"

I didn't know what to say. I said, "I love you" too because I did love him and I wanted him to know that but he never did anything like that before. In fact, he never really even said it. It was strange for him to go out of his way to come tell me that he loved me and nothing else.

Alex: *We couldn't really talk as much as we used to. We couldn't have as many intelligent and fun conversations because of his illness. But we still hung out on the couch like we used to with the dogs, Teddy and Bella.*

I never got frustrated with John. I felt compassion for him and sadness, because I knew how strong he had been but he was slowly being broken down by this disease. I expressed my frustrations most of the time by crying in my bed. I talked to myself a lot, yelled at God, blamed God, and hated God.

∂∾∾

John started therapy. Chemo and radiation. It had been just about forty days and forty nights since his surgery. And now, again, for just about forty days I transported John to the hospital for ten minutes of daily radiation. His chemo consisted of a pill he could take at home, which surprised me because of the potential danger it posed if anyone other than John so much as touched it. The chemo agent was so toxic that we were advised that we had to use a condom when we had sex. That, at least, was not a problem: we hadn't had sex in months, and I truly couldn't foresee any in the future. But John didn't share that vision, and insisted we stop at the first drugstore we passed after picking up the chemo pills to buy a box of condoms. Once the box was placed with care in a drawer in the bedside table, it remained untouched for the rest of John's life.

John remained physically strong throughout what seemed like an intensive, and somewhat fearsome, round of poisons coming from two different delivery systems aimed directly at his brain. But he didn't seem sick, weakened, not wiped out at all by the treatments. Though things were far from what normal once was, this was more normal than things had been for a long time. Except that John, who had once roamed the city at will, a freedom afforded to just about anyone over fourteen, stayed at home. He could focus at home. The world outside our property line threw too much input, too many distractions at him. With that he wouldn't be able to cope. Things wouldn't seem quite so familiar. Even small duties or trivial trips away from the house were nearly impossible for him to set a clear path through.

I'd had a trip to a bookstore planned, and John suddenly decided he wanted to accompany me. In the old days, I would have been thrilled. A little trip out could have wound up in a surprise intimate dinner, a possible movie, almost anything. But this request made my chest feel tight. To heck with it. I shook it off. It was a good sign that John wanted to get away from the house for a bit. Maybe we were edging a little closer to normal.

We made it to the store incident free. All right, I thought. This is good. This is sweet. John's movements weren't exactly fluid (he'd had some trouble getting into the car), but he was good enough for a bookstore. I stayed alongside him, though, not freewheeling through the store as I once would have. John suddenly stopped in front of one particular section sign. He looked at it for a moment or two, then back to me.

"What is fiction?" he asked, genuinely puzzled. "What does that mean?"

I felt the question register in my eyes, in the muscles of my face. "Fiction is stories. Not actual stories, but made up."

He held a book of fiction (to this day I think I refuse to remember the author or title) in his hand and looked at it like it was some arcane object. Eventually, I took it from him and placed it back on the shelf. I didn't realize he was looking at my face the entire time.

He said, "I'm sorry you're sad."

And, of course, I was. I could tell by the expression on his face that he could pair that emotion with the look on my face, but didn't really know what it meant, and couldn't feel that sensation himself.

I'm never surprised that I learn a thing or two in a bookstore. But this time it was learned not by words read in a book, but by two faces being read by two now very different people.

Chemotherapy and Radiation Therapy for Glioma

I don't know if I'm the first person to ever say this, or to put it down on paper, but I doubt it. I'm sure it's been muttered, hollered, and sighed by neuroscientists, neurologists, oncologists, and a few patients over the years: The brain-blood (or blood-brain, if you prefer) barrier, or the BBB as it's known in medical circles, is the Big Bad Bitch when one is trying to treat brain cancer. It consists of tightly joined cells that allow very few substances to travel into the brain, keeps most cells from traveling into the brain, and makes it extremely difficult to get medicine into the brain. To most molecules, including those of medications and treatments, the BBB says, "You aren't dressed right, you don't look right, and you don't act right to come in here." This is a problem if you have, say, glioblastoma multiforme and you'd like to have an oncologist, or someone of similar specialization deliver some medication try to stop your tumor from killing you. But the doorman that's been hired by evolution usually says, "Go anyplace you like—except in here." (Of course, you also have to give the BBB, in this case the Bold Beautiful Bodyguard, credit for keeping all manner of harmful substances from entering the brain. That, we can't complain about. It's a kind of Janus-faced entity, but without consciousness. It does what it does because it is the way it is.)

So treating glioma with chemotherapy is tricky. When John was receiving treatment, and right up to this day, there is exactly one drug specifically for glioma treatment: Temozolomide. Temodar—the drug's brand name—is a chemotherapeutic drug with the ability to cross the blood brain barrier. Why, you ask?

Because it can. And we're lucky it can. Because chemo alone can't cut the mustard. At least not by itself. And neither does radiation. But even temozolomide and radiotherapy rarely cure glioma; the combination doubles the median survival of patients, and that's not half bad.

The trouble is right now, glioma seems like it can't be totally vanquished by any means. An article on medscape.com states that the "median time to recurrence after standard therapy [that listed above] is 6.9 months."

The tenacity of glioma is in part due to the impossibility of removing all cancerous cells by surgery. There's too great a chance of doing brain damage that would make post-op life for the patient pointless. Even if 98 percent of a tumor is removed, that still leaves tens of millions of rogue cells in place, and chemo and radiation only wipes out or suppresses a portion of that which is left behind. And, as above, about seven months later, those cells start dividing again, and another tumor begins to grow.Treatment possibilities for recurrences are limited and not very effective. The primary treatment for recurring glioma is something called the Gliadel wafer (which was suggested for John, but more on that later). It's a treatment that's been around for eight years, but is not particularly effective, and creates other problems all by itself, such as blood clots and leakage of fluids into the brain, and other awful side effects.

A few clinical trials and experimental studies are going on now that use other drugs (Ukrain, a drug derived from alkaloids from the greater celandine plant and that is approved for use in a handful of countries overseas, supposedly has shown efficacy in treating cancers of the pancreas, breast, and colon; Swainsonine, an alkaloid of locoweed; and one of the most despised medications ever patented, thalidomide); new techniques (one in which a more focused radiation therapy is delivered directly to tumors through an implanted balloon that itself contains radioactive material); using not the polio vaccine, but the polio virus itself to attack the glioma cells, which seem to be susceptible to it; and immunizing patients against the cytomegalovirus (a very common but dangerous herpes virus), since most gliomas are infected with it. This last treatment mentioned has shown some promise in slowing tumor growth, but not in eradicating the cancer itself.

And despite research, and clinical trials, and the great goodwill of the medical community who fight cancer every day, survival times and rates for glioma patients have barely budged since this scourge was first identified.

I didn't know much of this until I began to write this book. These are things you wish you never had to know.

7.

John's treatments were over in six weeks, as promised. Three weeks later he started falling apart. Falling down. A lot. At first he could help me get him up if not on his feet, and least into a chair. But even that didn't last long, and then it was just me struggling to lift my big, forever-strong and handsome husband up from the floor.

John had seizures, many of them, and all he could do was sleep them off the way some ridiculous college binger would sleep off a big weekend. I watched him sleep, sometimes dozing off myself, then waking with a start, afraid that John wouldn't awaken at all.

I made the decision to take John back to Barrows ahead of schedule and insisted he have a scan done of his brain. The news the scan brought was not good. I hadn't expected it to be, of course, but I couldn't always trust my intuition anymore. (Other than from the kids, I wasn't expecting to see good coming from anything). Three new spots had formed on John's brain. In strictly physical terms, small. In medical and psychological terms, enormous. The glioma was recurring with remarkable speed. The cerebellum, where your physical coordination comes from, was the site of one of the new spots. That explained a lot. His motor skills were shot. The falling wasn't just weakness from the weeks of chemo and radiation. This was not something he would get over with time and rest.

The implantation of a Gliadel wafer was now brought up. Of course it would mean going into what should be no man's land—John's brain—once again. It was, in the most generous terms, a stopgap measure, one that might add some time to John's physical life, but would not in any way ensure any quality of life. And the side effects, as mentioned before, seemed almost more dreadful than the treatment.

After much discussion with John's parents, much to the dismay of his healthcare team at Barrows, we chose home instead. It was one of the most difficult decisions I've ever made, and I hope to never have to make a decision like that again. After weighing all the pros and cons I had before me, and after doing a lot of my own research I decided on a quality of life at home.

John didn't require much in the way of technical care. Just someone to be there, to do the things simple and complex that he no longer remembered having done, and no longer had the ability to do. We got up together every day. The kids spent time what time they could with him, trying to play simple games, stirring up memories, and sharing with him about their days at school and sports. But this was hard, emotional pounding my children shouldn't have to bob and weave through. There would be a lot of tough moments to content with coming up in the near future, but for me there was nothing more heartbreaking than seeing my children with the man who had been their big and strong father-figure not being able to play a small game with them, or even remember that he ever had.

I spent the days with John watching game shows on television. Every single day started with The Price is Right and ended with The King of Queens. There wasn't much in the way of communication, and when I tried to break the trance I was usually "shushed." Or, worse, on occasion John's disease made his mood utterly unpredictable, and he would chafe with angry frustration. I'd back off immediately. I couldn't be sure what was going through his mind, but I didn't want to make it any more troubling than it already was. This is not to give the impression that my thoughts, my actions were always saintly. I knew there was no point in expressing my frustrations or anger to John. He couldn't have understood the emotions storming through me. I don't believe he even understood he was losing his temper when he was doing it.

It was a frustrating and confusing time for all of us. When you're taking care of someone you love who is grievously, irreversibly ill, your own needs aren't necessarily as important. The patient is the purpose of every action, every decision. And more often than not becomes the only focal point of anyone involved in or witnessing the situation. It's not surprising. I guess that it's perfectly natural, and it seems perfectly unnatural to complain about it - for the caregiver to need some care, some attention.

Alex: I saw my mom go slowly insane. She was being broken down mentally and physically twice as fast as John was. I felt terrible, but there was nothing I could do. I tried consoling my mom and sister. I tried sucking it up, pretending I was fine, so they could see someone could do it and then they could do it. I knew I had to step up.I remember once I was in my mom and John's room once, and my Mom was crying to me. John walked in and she ran up and hugged him. He smiled and said, "Why are you crying? Don't cry I'm fine! It's OK, honey." While he was saying that I was standing behind my mom, and John looked at me and smiled. He gave me that look that just made me laugh and smile, and he slouched and dropped his arms, just making another joke. He knew I needed it. He knew how terrible it really was.My relationship with my mom just grew stronger during John's illness; because we all knew this would be the last time we would to be a family together. My mom, sister, and me became extremely close.

Caroline: I didn't realize the effect all this was having on my re- lationships with my friends or my schoolwork, but in seventh and eighth grades, my grades completely changed. I had been a straight- A student up until then, but after that my grades were really bad.

Alex: The whole situation didn't really mess up my schoolwork because I was always offered help whenever I felt I needed it.With my friends, I could tell they were trying to be nicer to me, but that just made things awkward. I didn't want them to feel bad for me. I just wanted them to be there for me. I felt more isolated because I was the only one going through anything like this. But I was still active with my life.

I was going through the motions of taking care of everybody, not necessarily taking care of myself. I compacted ten tons of emotional substance into the package of my body. And whether I knew it or not, I was setting myself up for a complete core meltdown in the very near future.

One other curious thing resulted from my being John's only caretaker. I felt I was becoming invisible. And despite the millions of fantasies people have entertained about invisibility, I can tell you that that experience, that sensation, was like nothing I had ever experienced and never cared to again.

Watching John struggling to succeed at ordinary feats such as feeding himself (and failing) was devastating to me. But after seeing it a half-dozen, two dozen times, I had to learn to diffuse my own misplaced exasperation, and at the same time I wanted him to maintain his dignity. I reminded myself that this wasn't his fault, this was not his choice. Who would choose to, say, have a broken leg for the sole purpose of forcing your loved ones to watch you struggle to tie your shoes? But even knowing that, and being careful to be mindful of my reactions, I still had to live with the unassailable idea that the man I loved, married, and hoped to spend my entire life with was no longer present.

God bless them, the doctors at Barrows kept trying to polish the smallest crystals of hope into diamonds. I listened to things such as, "He's holding steady" and "He could go for three more months, maybe three years, like this" as if they were witnessing encouraging signs of remarkable progress. They told us that we should not isolate ourselves and to socialize. Get out of town and relax, they told us. Not to live our lives as if our wheels were spinning in the sand.

I was... not overwhelmed with expectations, but I thought, all right, these people are among the best in the business. If they say we need to get out, that sensory stimulation would do us both good, I would give it a try. I owed John at least that much. I realized I, too, probably needed a break from what had become an almost crippling routine, but I didn't want to admit it to myself.So for the upcoming Memorial Day weekend, I planned for us a trip to meet some friends in Flagstaff. Though I'd been told John could fly, I knew what the pressure changes did to my ears, and I didn't even want to consider what they might do to John's head. I thought it best to drive.

People who haven't been to Arizona tend to think of it as flat, largely featureless desert. We have mountains and canyons—pretty grand ones—and we have towns that sit way up high. Like Flagstaff, which is at 6,910 feet, more than 1,600 feet higher than Denver. It's not uncommon for even healthy people to have a difficult time adjusting to a change from near sea level to that height. It is common for people to experience headaches and nausea when first arriving in Flagstaff.

Flagstaff turned out to be a nightmare for John.

I realized my mistake as soon as John, Alex, Caroline and I arrived, but had no idea of the seriousness of it. I thought it might just be the usual adaptation people go through as I detailed above. But John's fragility was only amplified by the mountains. God, I thought to myself, can I do anything right?

But John, even though he must have been able to sense his increased frailty, wanted to stay. We went out to meet our friends for dinner. As we walked into the restaurant, John suddenly just crumpled. I was able to catch him before he hit the ground. He was stable, though weak, so we continued inside. But as soon as we were heading for the table, I was sorry we had left the house in Phoenix. His body was still trembling, he wasn't speaking right, and he had an odd look on his face.

Alex and the husband of a friend of ours helped John back to the car. His right leg was dragging. He couldn't talk anymore, or really walk, either. We returned to our rented weekend retreat immediately.

John slept peacefully through the night, with me wide awake at his bedside, crying, wrecked, and watching for any sign of distress or disaster. I had called the hospice nurse, and she said that John probably had a stroke. He awoke in the morning, groggy, but alive and intact.

One of my friends who was visiting Flagstaff, a doctor, took a look at John and said that the elevation was probably just too much for him, and that we needed to head to familiar lower ground.

The kids insisted that I not drive, so that I could keep an eye on John. So one of our friends drove us back to Phoenix. John wouldn't or couldn't talk. He seemed to be disappearing as he slept in his seat. I nodded in affirmation at every road sign that marked a drop in elevation. When we finally reached a significantly lower altitude, John started to seem a bit better.

We arrived home and got John situated in our bedroom. My doctor friend had warned me to be prepared. This might be the beginning of the end for John. I called a nurse from hospice, who came out to monitor John's vital signs. I was finally able to collapse for a little while into a chair next to the bed.

I held my head in my hands, trying not to think, trying not to judge myself too harshly for taking a trip to the mountains. It would have been nothing a year ago. A quick zip up to Flagstaff, a great weekend, then home again, how bad could it be? But this was now, not a year ago, not even a matter of a couple of months ago, before John's surgery.

I was freaked out, and rightfully so. At this moment I was terrified at the thought of changing any small thing in John's environment. He slept for what seemed like two days straight. And whether it was an entirely conscious decision or not, we hunkered down in the house and went nowhere for weeks. During that time we gathered as a family in our home, which included John's parents and his older children, to be there in support of John and one another.

Alex: I never blamed any person for what I saw happening: not myself, my mom, my sister, not anyone. I blamed God. It was not fair what happened to John. It was the most unfair thing to happen to anyone ever. Everyone loved John. And God killed him. John never acted differently toward me, even though he obviously was not himself. But at the same time he was himself because you could always tell what John was trying to do or say. You could still see the John Graves that everyone knew and loved.

There was an obvious wall between us, though. We were no longer as close as we had been. We could no longer talk about sports together and talk about shows, because he could not say what he wanted. I always tried to ask questions that just needed yes or no answers or a head nod or rhetorical questions, because it hurt me to see him like that.I came home one morning after staying the night at a friend's, and I was very angry with my sister. I was going to yell at her, and John stood in front of me in the hallway to try to stop me. I just walked by; he couldn't hold me back. He was much bigger than me, almost six foot five, but he could not hold me back. The strongest man I had ever known could no longer stop me. I broke down.

8.

Haircuts. We could go get haircuts. This was not the equivalent of the historic moment when The Beatles decided they would get haircuts and inevitably change hairstyle history forever. But this was something we could do. Something we could accomplish.

That was my first impulse to leave the house for days and days and days that I could possibly obey.

Chemotherapy and radiation had not been kind to John's hair. It was present in sort of oily patches, shabby. It seemed to go whichever the way the wind blew, even if we were inside. I was hoping to bring a little joy to him, make him as pleased as he could be with the man he saw in the mirror.

Sitting in the chair at the hair salon, the man in the mirror looked exhausted, the life drained out of him. The short walk to get into the car, then to exit at the stylist had been too much exertion for John. The stylist obviously knew he was being called on to perform some magic on John's behalf. But there was just no helping what had once been a fine head of hair. Sadly, John looked a little more diminished after the experience, and I have held that largely meaningless episode in my heart and have not been able to let it go.

It was becoming more and more difficult to meet John's needs at home. I just couldn't keep up. As he became less able to function, my ability to rise to the occasion was decreasing. I had to broach a subject I'd hoped I'd never to have to speak of: inpatient hospice care.

The work done at hospices is more than magic: it is miraculous. The care with which they provide people who don't have much time left on this earth is stunning. The people who perform this work are a breed apart. I know I can't account for every single one, but I've found most to be among the more sensitive human beings you'll ever meet.

As soon as I mentioned hospice care to John, the familiar but lately largely absent belligerent John made his presence known again. The nurse and social worker from hospice who stopped by weekly asked me if I'd brought up the subject with John. I told them I had, but there was no way he would go. He was absolutely adamant about not leaving the house.

"Let us give it a try," the nurse said, "see if we can make a little headway on the subject." They went to speak with John in the other room. I sat down, looked out the window, counting the seconds until they returned in the wake of his ill- tempered, intemperate response. They walked back into the room. Did I even look up? I don't recall. But I did when I heard this: "He said he's fine with it."I was too wasted emotionally and physically to ask how they'd gotten him to agree. That is, if he actually seemed to understand what they were talking about. I'd have to discover that for myself as subtly as possible later. I nodded my head, grateful. If I'd had been capable of it, I would have hugged them. But they seemed to understand that, and weren't disappointed that the modest dip of my head was all I could offer.

On a particular day, one that probably didn't seem much different than the day before to most people in Phoenix, in the country, in the world, I said to my husband, "We need to move you to hospice, honey. It's a better place for you to be now. They'll take really good care of you, and I will be there the whole time."

This was as gut-wrenching as anything I'd ever said to anyone. I was aching, exhausted. I was made of rubber and bendy straws.

John's response was this: "I'm not going anywhere. I want to stay home."

Suddenly I was one great exposed nerve, twanging and tight.

Shortly thereafter their transport service had arrived, and John, not happy but not capable of displaying much of a reaction, got into the wheelchair they'd brought into the house and was wheeled toward the van. One terrible sight from that terrible moment remembered: John's foot dragging, nearly getting caught in the wheel of the chair because he could not move it out of the way. That was heart–wrenching for me. Besides that sad small mishap, John was placed peacefully, though awkwardly, into the van and went off to hospice, with me seated behind him.

Hospice. This particular hospice had been highly recommended to us, but did not sit well with me from the moment I walked in. This hospice was not a place of miracles. It was awful. I didn't know anything about the people who worked inside, but I couldn't imagine why anyone would agree to so much as walk inside. I did, and I relive that dreadful visit we had from time to time. It didn't seem so much like a place to care for the dying as it did a sort of secure unit for unhealthy semi-ne'er-do-wells, somewhere you'd bring a misbehaving uncle to show him the horrors of what prison life could be like, so he'd bring to a halt the activities that could lead him there.

As horrible as it was, we stayed an entire night. The next morning I grabbed my phone and started dialing. If I couldn't find a place for John at least a thousand times better than this, I was determined to take him home. But luck or the Norse gods or the offensive line of the Arizona Cardinals was on my side during those calls. I did find space in The Sherman Home, run by Hospice of the Valley, in a facility a world away from where we had just come. Truly, the Four Seasons of hospice care.

Even though the staff hadn't had to imagine the existence of anyone named John Graves until a few minutes before our arrival, he was greeted as if they'd been waiting for him for months, as if there were to be a party that could not start without him. He was not a man with a death sentence galloping hard toward him, but a visitor fit and healthy at a lovely guesthouse where all his needs would be tended to. He was, to my joy, and John's I think, dubbed "The Handsome Guy," and all the women on staff went out of their way to help him and feel that that wonderful moniker they'd bestowed on him was not just the truth for me, but an undeniable fact to them as well.

I was with John at The Sherman Home as close to always as I could be. He was sleeping nearly 24/7 now. Sometimes I got into bed with him. I hope he could sense my body against him. The feeling of him breathing next to me was so comforting. And when he would reflexively slip his arm around me, it evoked one of the most intense sensations of bliss I'd ever experienced.

John was at hospice for only three days before he lost fully his ability to speak. Sometimes he would open his mouth and attempt to speak, but he couldn't find his words, his voice.

Caroline: *At first the visits were kind of… awkward. I just didn't really know what was going on, what to do, how to react or what to say. John's relatives were usually all there as well, and I just had never dealt with something like this before so I didn't know what to do. He seemed very quiet and tired. He didn't really understand what was going on, just like me!*

He recognized me right away at the beginning, but near the end it took him a while to realize who I was. Sometimes, I don't even know if he actually knew. I think he just acted like he did out of embarrassment. Like when my mom would say "It's Caroline," he would just agree and pretend he was "with it."

There was one particular visit when I went to visit him, in hospice I think, and we were all standing around his bed—my mom, Alex, and me—and after chatting, or trying to, we were saying our good-byes. He grabbed my hand, looked at me, smiled and asked, "Will I see you tomorrow?" And I said, "Yes, you will," and then we left. I have never, ever, forgotten that moment because I never saw him again. I never came back "tomorrow" like I said I would.

Alex: *I visited John once when he was at Barrows before he had surgery. He was the same John I had always known, same comedian, and still put smiles on everyone's face. I visited him once when he was at hospice. That was a week before he died. I never went back because before I left he said "I love you" and I said it back, and that was the best way it could have ended. I regret not going everyday to see him. But I know that would have made it worse. It was the hardest decision I've ever made and I will never forget it.*

At Barrows he recognized me immediately; at hospice it took him several minutes to recognize me even though he immediately said "Hey." I knew he didn't know who I was until a little while later. I never tried talking to him at the hospital about things that would belittle or embarrass him for not being able to respond about them.

He was not breathing easily. It was irregular, and it rattled me to the bone.By the time Alex and Caroline came to say farewell to their Great Big Dad he could no longer move his arms or legs. Alex and Caroline were good; better than good. They were stronger than anyone their age should have been able to be. But I knew they would be imprinted for the rest of their lives by what they were experiencing here.

For the two days following, John did nothing, could do nothing, but stare straight ahead. I cannot imagine what he was feeling, thinking, seeing. Maybe John was getting a glimpse of that mystery – that we will all come to experience. But I would just as soon hope that the ultimate vision doesn't last as long for us as it did for John.

It was the next day day, July 7, 2007—7, 07, 007—when John reached the Unfinished Line. The end of a life incomplete, so much left undone. My Handsome Husband. Big Daddy. John Graves from a little town in Iowa, moved to the great American desert. Found a lot of love. Found some heartache. The great human experiment, the great human experience. Which always ends the same way for everyone. With a great breath out, and then nothing to follow behind.

Caroline: I was in my mom's bed the morning John died. My stepsister Erinn was there and woke me up and said, "He died."

I got out of bed and went to my room. I was with all of his kids who were crying and just complete wrecks. For some reason, I couldn't cry. I wanted to, because I felt like I should. I felt weird that I wasn't crying. And even when I first saw John's entire family at hospice crying, I still didn't cry. I felt like it wasn't my place to be sad. Even though that is untrue and ridiculous. At that moment I felt like I was just his stepdaughter among all of his blood relatives. My turn to cry would come later, after all of them had the chance to let it out. I don't know why I felt this way.

Then I went to hospice with everyone and that's when it finally broke. I started weeping really hard.

Alex: *When I visited John at hospice I understood that he was going to die. I knew it was coming soon, but I didn't realize how soon. A couple of days before, I was at the movies with a friend and Caroline called me. She was crying, and told me that John was breathing loud and really hard, and how bad things were. That's when I knew it was going to happen in the next few days.*

On July 7th I was in bed very early in the morning. Erinn came in and told me he passed away and asked if I wanted to go to hospice. I told her I didn't want to go, and I stayed in bed and tried to fall back to sleep. Of course I couldn't. But I didn't cry, either. I thought about everything that was going to be different now. I thought about how my role was going to change.

I didn't cry until later that day when my mom came home and I finally saw her for the first time in days. She gave me the biggest hug ever; she started to cry and then I was in tears too.

After John died my life didn't change very much immediately. No one really seemed to believe it. Our house was no longer the same. It was not a loving and fun house; it was depressing and sad.

Since John died, I've never been myself again. That's one thing that did change right away. I had help from a few friends that I was extremely close with. But I didn't really want help. In my freshman year of high school after John passed away I had a hard time at school, because someone would say something or do something that would remind me of him. I spent a lot of time with my dogs because they were closer to John than any of us. He loved them more than any man loved anything. And I saw him when I looked at and spent time with them. They helped me more than anything.

My mom, Caroline, and I stopped being the same family that we had been pretty soon after John died. We were no longer united. My relationship with my mom changed drastically.

At the very beginning, nothing much changed and we were all still very close, and I was still sucking it up so that they could see me being strong. I hoped it would help them. But Caroline isolated herself and didn't un-isolate herself from me for a very long time. She seemed to have some kind of hatred for me. I lost most of my respect for her because she wouldn't get angry with my mom for the wrong decisions she was making. Caroline would agree with me when I would talk about it, but as soon as I brought those things up with my mom Caroline would backtrack and pretend like she had no idea what I was talking about.

Then after a few months I began to despise my mom. I could not stand her. I hated her. I hated her decisions, I hated the things she said, I hated what she wore, who she talked to, I hated everything about her. I lost all respect for her when she began to date so soon after John had died.

Part Two
That's All She Wrote
9.

I was completely unsprung, a fragile, smashed wristwatch that had been designed to wind itself on the energy of the slightest human vibration. I could no longer sense the soft hum of the subtle machinery working inside me. Either everything was on strike, or I was completely out of the "being" business.

I was still holding on to John. Hugging his body to mine. All I could think was that if I didn't let go, if I didn't leave, they couldn't take him away. I knew this body was not John anymore. That divine creation was much, much more than this poor spent form I was clinging to. But I knew that as soon as I loosened myself and walked out of the room, they would be taking him away, to a place where no more decisions needed to be made. There was no more what-to-do-next; this man I had loved had no future. Truthfully, for the forty-five minutes or so I laid there, he had no present either. Time and travel belonged to only one of us, and I didn't want it.

I did reluctantly let him go, muscle by individual muscle. I said my final good-bye, to whom or what or where, I don't know. And I took the forever journey that was the trip to a home that was until an hour ago "ours"; to a new place that was "mine." At that moment, that felt like the ugliest word in the world. The old saying that possession is nine-tenths of the law may be true, but it has no value whatsoever when you never wanted this particular form of possession to begin with.

ॐ ॐ

All of John's children came home that night; the ones who currently lived there, those who had lived here at one time, and those who never had. But this was home to all of them for at least one night. We did what I suppose people the world over do: we told stories, talked nonsense, we laughed and we cried. Nothing is ever the same about the particulars of anyone's loss, but it seems to me also that there exists a level where everything is the same, and that's what makes this world what it is. Some commonality of emotion and experience.

I don't know why, but after the first, short part of the evening, all assembled found ourselves talking about nothing but the future. We certainly couldn't have run out of tales to tell. Maybe we had become exhausted over the last few months and needed to think of what was coming instead of what we'd lost, and inevitably, at least physically, left behind. But the first thing in all of our immediate futures was John's funeral and memorial service. They needed to be planned, and I was in no shape to be myself, to jump in and take charge and knock out the details.

My dearest friends helped me plan both events. When I realized Caroline and I didn't have black dresses, another friend took us to buy them. I think it would have been the worst shopping trip in the world if Caroline and I had had to do it ourselves. Buying a simple black dress became an awful task to be completed as quickly as possible, and then forgotten twice as fast. We were in a daze, not quite yet to the stage of self-protective selective memory, but approaching it with no understanding that we were heading there.

The memorial service at All Saints was standing room only. I don't recall much on that day, but I do remember feeling John's presence in the limo on the way over to the service. Alex had been holding himself together the whole time John was sick, and that day he was completely inconsolable. He unraveled. Everything else was just a blur...

৵৽

Two days after the service, reality showed up in the form of a phone call from the office. Oh, yeah, I own a business. The supervisor I'd hired to take care of Villa Pavers while I was tending to John was hounding me to get back to work and to get back quickly. Where was I, he wanted to know. What was I doing? This is your business, he reminded me, and you need to pay it some serious attention.

I thought about asking permission of my own staff to have two fucking days to move past my husband's death. But sarcasm never turns out to be a truly good friend (sometimes a momentary highly satisfying pal you later come to regret knowing), and so I took my mind off "stunned" and headed for the office at warped speed...

... Straight into a storm of meteors.

Or, more precisely, meet-eors, because from the moment I arrived back at my office at Villa Pavers everything was chaos, and all we had were meetings, meetings, meetings. All with an unexpected overtone of hostility aimed directly at me. I have to admit, I was taken by surprise. I did not play the "Poor Me" role when I came back to business, but still there was serious resentment that I hadn't been paying attention to our business, while I was doing all I could for John and our family.

There was a kind of surreal lack of acknowledgment that John, who until his trip to Tucson, had been one of their two employers, had suffered a terrible illness and death. And I didn't feel it was my place to … well, demand some respect, or at least some notice, of his painful, final journey.

OK, I thought, we're not family. We're a business. And as a business we were in trouble. People panic when trouble they've seen on the horizon tornadoes into their front yard. That's about where we were, and coupled with everyone in paycheck-protection mode, that's where the stress and anxiety were coming from.

But talk, talk, and more talk was not going to turn my company, or any company, back onto the right course. Though we could not have known it at the time, the Great Recession was coming, and one of the first spots it would come down hard would be Phoenix.

I thought, *I have to keep this place going. I cannot let the business John and I built fail.*

In the movies, when a character utters the clichéd "Failure is not an option" line, you know it really is not an option. No film producer in existence is going to let a screenwriter or director let a nation of millions watch a star worth billions fail in his or her mission, impossible or not.

But I was the star of this movie, and it was a stinker. I had no film studio backing me up. I had a hostile to semi-hostile staff, and a supervisor—the cousin of a friend of mine—who seemed content to watch the ship sink until I could get back on deck to direct it straight to the bottom.

Maybe I had been gone too long. *Had* I been grieving too long? OK, I thought, the business is viable. But some things had to change. First, and maybe most unfortunately, people were getting paid too much, particularly my supervisor. I was not only not being overpaid; I was paying myself nothing at all. I couldn't afford myself unless I got this place back on the beam.

In one sense, this was a good thing. I could not dwell on John's death or what I'd done to care for him over the previous five-and-a-half months. Now I was charged with taking care of something we'd created together, and I became all about keeping Villa Pavers a going concern. I was thinking sustainability; personal and professional. I was not thinking, *I need time to heal. I may not quite be ready for this.* I could not afford that.

I hit the autopilot feature in my head. (It's not so much a button as it is a… oh, heck, let's think of it as a button.) I knew I was being perceived as someone who no longer cared about her business. So I did everything I thought I should do. I pushed myself and allowed myself to be pushed. Whatever I thought needed to be done I did; whatever anyone else thought needed to be done, I also did. The business had not been running right since John began to have his inexplicable symptoms. He had been making a lot of wrong decisions and all the wrong moves. Simultaneously, as you know, I was making a lifetime's worth of incorrect assumptions.

While I had been accusing John of gambling, having a drug addiction, or anything that would have explained where the money was going, I later learned that we were losing money because of simple business oversights, such as uninvoiced jobs, unsupervised crews and unexplained materials disappearing.

I tried not to beat myself up for what I'd done. Particularly not with a staff that was making me feel as if I didn't belong in my own company. But of course I did belong here. This place was all John and me, and I found reminders of him every day in the office. A handwritten note posted here, a file on one of his clients parked on a chair over there. It was hard, but I had to block it out as if it were noise. If I could reduce that clamor to a whisper, I could think straight.

I hired Arleen, a wonderful woman who knows numbers like she invented them. Though she was not a cleanup woman, by any stretch of the imagination, the first thing she helped me do was "clean house." It was time to make a change in staff. It was necessary. As you might guess, it was not pleasant, but nothing over the last half year had been. I then hired a smaller staff—through no grand design, I hired all women to run what one would think of as a male-centric industry. They were the finest team I could have assembled, and we did excellent work with the materials and the marketplace we had. But the recession was not going to leave us alone because we needed it to. Our business had cliff-dropped from eight crews working full time to no crews working on no jobs. New building activity and home renovations in Phoenix hit the brakes so hard, the city briefly skidded into New Mexico.

Companies in the building trades were folded fast and sloppy, like construction-paper origami at an angry kid's birthday party. And, since numbers don't lie (per Arleen), it was becoming abundantly clear that we were soon destined to become just a nasty shape stained with dirty fingers too.

Even though I knew the larger truths of what was going on in the world, I was devastated. I took the recession personally. I couldn't do anything right. *Can't save the business*, I said to myself. Couldn't save John, I thought to myself in my weak moments. It was all wrapped up together. It had been my beautiful package, and I'd let it all slip away. If I'd been thinking clearer, I might have correctly concluded that at least a massive regional depressive crash was coming. But I was snagged in the details. Liquidating inventory. Selling trucks at a loss. And saying good-bye to the magnificent women of Villa Pavers, the last, best crew I'd ever have.

To shield myself against a total meltdown for the three months it would take to shut down the business, I got numb. Numb is still a feeling though. And after all I'd already come through, I thought it was the worst one I could have at the time. I was wrong.

Because then I got dumb.

The 0, 5, or 7 Stages of Grief

Grief is at least an absolutely undeniable human condition. (Biologists report observing this condition in other animals as well, including geese, elephants, dolphins, and dozens of other animals.) You might experience it early in life (though I tremble at the thought of a child having to work through such a devastating and complex emotional episode) or not until later in life, when people expect you to be old or mature enough to "handle it." There is no handling grief. It is complex, every color at once, and shrouded in the mystery that is the unique inner life of every individual. Even observing someone else's sense of intense grief can be a terrible life-changing experience, and some people will go as far as they can to insulate themselves from that, consciously putting as much distance between themselves and anyone going through it.

But grief is everywhere, and distance from one sufferer, though unintentionally, brings you closer to another. If you are in this world, you cannot just walk away from it.

John and I each experienced profound grief during his illness. But though the "stages" of grief carry the same names for a dying person as they do for the caretaker of that person, one's role in that terrible drama makes the experience of grief a different character.

There have been decades of debate over grief and bereavement. The first and most famous concept of the "stages" theory of grief came from Elisabeth Kubler-Ross's *On Death and*

Dying. She put forward a five-stage theory of grief, which related to the state of mind of a person with a terminal illness (though it could be applied, less directly, to the loved ones of that person). While John was going through his ultimate crisis, and I was trying to shepherd him through as painlessly as possible, I didn't have the chance to stop to consider what might be playing out in John's mind. Though his thinking, of course, was impaired first by the tumor itself, and then by the various drastic treatments he endured, it didn't necessarily mean he wasn't experiencing profound sorrow on a real and deep level. He may not have been able to express those feelings, but looking back, a good bit of his behavior mirrored the stages that Kubler-Ross identified.

Though her theory has been supported, debunked, satirized, disparaged, appended, and diluted since it was first published forty-plus years ago, my own personal experience tells me it still deserves some respect and consideration. How many of his reactions were caused by the tumor pressure, then the surgery, on his frontal lobe no one will ever know. But the five stages of grief Kubler-Ross identified—denial, anger, bargaining, depression, and acceptance—mirrored John's outward reactions to his care, the demands placed on him, the situations he faced (which he had virtually no control over), even some of the simple things I or his family and doctors asked of him that he could have, theoretically, performed or agreed to easily enough.

John may well have understood the early signs of his illness, at least enough to be apprehensive about them, and tried to deny those symptoms, which would have delayed the discovery of the brain tumor. Truthfully, with glioma patients, early discovery and treatment of a tumor does not necessarily add to a person's survival time or the relative success of that person's treatment. John's case was hopeless from the moment it began. But he could not have known that, and it was only natural that he would attribute common symptoms such as eye discomfort, headaches, forgetfulness, and other early signs as something relatively benign. People who claim that every small sick feeling they have is caused by a significant, possibly deadly, illness are generally looked at as either hypochondriacs or hopelessly neurotic.

I can't claim that John experienced a steady march through the five stages in military order (Kubler-Ross herself said that some of the stages might not even be experienced by most people, and it would surely be pure happenstance if a person did experience them in the exact lineup and intensity Kubler-Ross first wrote about). But I did come to recognize some of John's behavior in the descriptions of those stages, and it made me question my early conclusion that his actions were caused solely by damage to his brain and by the steroids he later took.

Since the publication of *On Death and Dying* other writers, scientists, and grief specialists have come up with their own theories of grief, defining not only scenarios for the patients but for the people who love them as well. There's a seven-stage theory, a no-stage theory, maybe even a six-dimensional theory, but they all have certain elements, and certain truths as I experienced them, in common. Shock and denial, of course, when you first discover the one you love, with whom you've planned a detailed and remarkable future with, will not be on that lifelong journey with you. That thought is devastating enough—and that's just the first sign, stage, or whatever term you'd prefer. It's the beginning, and it's not a starting spot anyone wants to be standing on, waiting for the rest of the process to unfold.

To me, one of the least-talked about and least-understood aspects of grief is the fact that it has very, very long legs: a terrible spider. The realization of what's happened to you, the one left behind, may not hit you until eight months to a year after your loved one's death. This is about the time when most friends and family think you should start coming out of mourning. In reality, you're just finally coming to a full understanding of what's occurred, and that's when the true grieving begins.

Grief is ultra real. It is complicated. It displays itself to different people in different ways. People need to learn to respect it. Not to try to jolly someone out of it. It doesn't work. It's not a sprint, it's a marathon you can't carbo-load for. But if you yourself are experiencing true grief, and you feel it's going on too long or you don't feel right about your thoughts or actions, see someone you can trust for help.

That's important. It's imperative .

Live through the grief, don't try to go around it. Then, though it is easier said and written than done, live your life.

10.

When the wheels come off of anything—a stroller, a car, a career—most people stop pushing or driving the thing. They have the sense, the perspective, the perceptive capabilities to hear the object scraping along the ground, making an ungodly grind.

I had lost the wheels and the axles on my life, but I kept my foot on the gas, held the steering wheel in a kind of death grip, and imagined I knew exactly where I was going. But in hindsight I see now that I was in overdrive on a road I'd never traveled down before.

Advice to readers: When something you're driving is shooting out sparks, get out of the thing and take a look underneath. If you see your past, present, and future under there, take a little time to think about your situation.

But I didn't want to know, I didn't want to hear, I didn't want to see.

In early November, just about four months after John passed away, some friends took me to dinner one evening. (Good friends are always kind to the walking wounded.) During a lull in the conversation, I went up to the bar to talk to the restaurant manager. Tarbell's had always been a favorite of John's and mine, and we considered the manager if not a close friend, at least an enjoyable and interesting acquaintance. We spoke for a little while, until he had to excuse himself to tend to one of his million tasks of the day. As he left, a man sitting at the bar asked if he could buy me a drink. To my small (and brief) credit, my defensive armor was immediately activated.

This guy, though, seemed to know me. At least a little about me. He knew where my son went to school. I asked him how, and he said he'd seen me around at different social and charitable functions. He followed with, "I saw you at LGO the other day [a local coffee house I used to frequent] and noticed that you were wearing a wedding band on your left hand. But now you're not."

That was pretty perceptive--and accurate. Two days before I'd switched my rings from my left hand to my right. I told him to hold on for just a minute and went back to my table to caucus with my friends. I described the situation. They said, "Look, if you feel comfortable with it, go ahead. It's just a drink, but be careful."

And so I let M. (needless to say, a pseudonym, or pseudo-initial) buy me a drink. It was only a brief time since the terrible events had played out in my life But I hadn't had the opportunity to process what had happened, having been yanked out of grieving mode and back into the business swamp I thought my absence had created. And I was surprised and flattered and relieved in a way by the attention.

M. was smart and very smooth. And I'd never seen a vampire in the desert before, much less at one of my favorite restaurants. We had a drink. Just one.

Then he called me. The next day. And I fell, as if the floor I was standing on was made of rice paper. Just being near him charged every cell in my body. The attraction was undeniable. It was instant and intense, and it was the biggest mistake I'd ever make. (Well, so far. I still have potential and plenty of years ahead of me to make even worse judgments.)

We saw each other during the day, and then again every night. He promised he'd help me work out of the morass that the business had become. He promised me the moon and the stars. He promised me that our life together would be nothing but bliss. And, I believed him because I wanted to believe that my life could be nothing short of amazing after what I had just been through.

Whatever it is that people say about the Wisdom of Children is probably mostly B.S. But in this case, my kids were dead-on, because they despised M. on sight. Whether it was out of allegiance to John or being unprepared to accept anyone else into our tightly woven family circle, or their personal experiences of having already seen vampires in the desert, they knew. Boy, did they know.

M. was smooth as silk. He knew just what to say and how to say it, and he knew how to manipulate people, so that he always stayed in control. This generous, kind-hearted, thoughtful, giving person also had the ability to be the cruelest, most conniving, mean-spirited man I had ever encountered. His M.O. was to play head games with me, and leave me feeling so insignificant and insecure, that I found myself turning back to him for validation and reassurance. This was our dance. He was a gentleman, a businessman, a cowboy, a sailor, a romantic; but mostly he was an imposter portraying the role of someone who actually cared for me. To this day, I'm sure he would maintain that he does care. I, however, am certain that our definitions of the word "care" would not be compatible.

I was swept up so quickly I didn't realize I'd also been instantly pocketed like loose change. The kids' objections I wrote off to oversensitivity. And though I tried to ignore it, they not only despised M., but they quickly came to despise me as well. (Thank God, only temporarily. They were and are more forgiving than anyone should be.) They had a perfect view of this "relationship," seats right on the fifty-yard line, with no one standing up to cheer and blocking their unobstructed line of sight. They were right to not like what they saw, and they had the guts to tell me. I just didn't have the guts to listen.

I don't know what it must feel like to watch someone you love being manipulated toward a bad end by someone and not being able to do anything about it. But I know what it feels like to be manipulated by a master of the art. It feels great and terrible. The more odious the manipulation techniques, the better tools it offers you to suppress the terrible feelings and hop from one nightmare to the next, with seemingly no knowledge of past transgressions, no matter how colossal and new.

M. had gone through a nasty divorce. He shared with me that he had been unfaithful to his wife for a long time before she had discovered his infidelity. He told me that he now understood how wounding his behavior had been, and that he would never behave that way with anyone again. He was in the process of ending his bond with the woman he had had the affair with, washing his hands of her. After he pulled his Pontius Pilate, he'd be all mine, he assured me. What a catch.

Um… yeah. For the exact amount of time we were in each other's physical presence. I didn't know it at first: that first affair continued all through our whatever you'd want to call it. I shudder to say relationship or any other word that seems to legitimize what I was doing. Because even when I discovered that his other involvement was continuing, I stayed with him. I got played perfectly: I can't deny that. When a fish is on a hook, they at least have the sense of self-preservation to try to get rid of it. I took the hook and lived for the pull of it. I don't know who I was, what I had become.

It seemed as if I wasn't even part of the greater emotional equation here: Everything had to be about M. I couldn't even grieve for John because there was no room for it in this polluted soap bubble I was living in. Why wasn't this a tip-off to me? Was I nuts? I suppose so.

For a while I was. I can admit it now. I sure didn't want to then.

Everyone who knew me, including my dearest Alex and Caroline, kept trying to warn me about what I was becoming. But when they'd hold up a mirror for me to look into, I'd just make sure my hair looked good for M. and then go meet him somewhere for dinner and after-dinner festivities.Even during our dinners and the aftermath, Affair Girl was his shameless and open obsession. We had to talk about her all the time. (For the briefest of brief moments, I wasn't sure if he was involved with her or if I was.) He was breaking up with her but wanted to remain friends. He needed to talk to her and get things straight. M. actually left my bed in tears one evening to fly to her to "make things right."

Yep. Make things right. With Affair Girl. While I was lying there. I raised myself up on an elbow to watch my mind and self-respect walk out the door hand-in-hand behind him.

Once more, he returned to town, assuring me, Clueless Catherine, that his relationship with Affair Girl was "over and done."

For Christmas he showered me with almost a dozen presents. I was so thrilled with them until the moment that I discovered that he and Affair Girl had exchanged Christmas gifts themselves. I wound up throwing each and every one of them at him while in hysterical tears later in the day.

I didn't even have the comfort of being in my own home, where I could order him out. Where I lived with my kids. Where I'd lived with a wonderful husband I'd wrongly suspected of having had an affair. And I was still in the messy process of closing down Villa Pavers.

No one in my life wanted to be near him. Not my friends, not my kids. (Who, to my forever discredit, I made come on a "family trip" with us. I still shudder when I think about that, and I mouth a silent apology to Alex and Caroline.) Not the people who worked for me, no one in my or John's family. Proximity was not at a premium.

And I could have reached up and removed the hook anytime I wanted. I wasn't paralyzed, at least not in the traditional sense. But, I didn't want to. I was punishing myself, I think. I couldn't save John. I didn't do enough for him. I'd failed in every way, I'd think, and then M. would make those thoughts fly from my head because I could only think of him and his life, which was the great important thing in this imitation of a relationship. A relationship that continued on and off for a year.

I may have had some sort of dreadful smile on my face as I farewelled my friends and family, watched them recede into the distance. It had moved past the scene of a bad car accident; they simply could not witness any more of my self-destruction. But, I was determined to make this love connection work. I would not screwup this massive screwup. I had invested immense amounts of energy in this person, and I surely wasn't ready to lose another man. Life energy that I didn't realize was truly in short supply. It couldn't be for nothing. It all had to be real.

My behavior, I realize now, was truly abhorrent. I had become Crazy Girl. (If there is ever a comic book called Crazy Girl vs. Affair Girl, the rights are mine. I lived it. I earned them. All proceeds will be donated to the people I damaged.) Watch me throw presents while tears fountain from my eyes. Watch me make excuses for every creepy thing M. did, with my knowledge and without, sometimes with my blessing. Watch Catherine Graves disappear before your very eyes.

No. On second thought, avert your gaze. This wasn't something any feeling person would ever want to witness.

Then finally, after the year of living dangerously, or an *annus horribilis* or whatever phrase you'd prefer for living through the dumbest year of your life, somehow miraculously my sense and sensibilities started to function again. I began to question what I was doing to myself, what I was doing to the people I loved (some of whom I would lose for good as a result of that year), and just who this life-sucking human weapon was that I'd chosen to cause my self-destruction.I found a little deposit of strength left deep within and tapped it. I walked away. But it was not easy and I didn't get away clean. I would end up needing the kind of help I thought I'd never need.

I had jammed myself, and all along I really thought I had it all under control. Not quite. This was my life and my mistake. And now my time had come to take back some control and regain my dignity.

11.

Food can trigger allergy attacks. Food can trigger bulimic episodes, anorexic panics, hiatal-hernia backflow, burning sensations, tongue numbness, bad breath… But, when food, in this case ketchup, the lost wonder vegetable of the Reagan Administration, triggers a five-day, nonstop, fetal-curled crying jag, you get the feeling that there might be a larger, major malfunction afoot.

I should have, at worst, been having a benign, all-but-silent interaction with a half-dozen condiment bottles in my cupboard. I knew we were up to our ears in ketchup. Ditto mustard, mayo, and just about every other standard bottled, bagged, and canned kitchen staple. But on this day the ketchup, the damned ketchup, caught my eye and froze me in place as if it were a loaded shotgun pointed right at my heart. Since John's death, something in me wanted to be sure to have enough, and more than enough, of everything my little family might need. And the ketchup reminded me that we were a little family, minus One. Alex, Caroline, and

I were a little pack that stood together against the world, with schoolbooks and ketchup …and the gut-smashing truth of John's passing inside our hearts and heads.

I started to cry.

I couldn't stop.

I couldn't move.

And then I did move. To the darkness and solitude of my bed, and spent the better part of the following week in my signature shallow, now-solo, dent in the king-size mattress.

I knew on some level, this was a bad sign. But I wasn't listening to myself just then. Nor was I listening to much of anyone.

The kids came home from school that first day, and wondered if I was sick.

"Wiped," I said. "That's all. Just need to sleep for a while."

The next morning, when I hadn't moved from the position I'd been in when Alex and Caroline had come home from school the previous day, Caroline made an executive decision worthy of someone much beyond the typical eighth-grader. She brought me the phone. My best friend, Gretchen, was on the line.

"When someone says they'll call me back, and they don't call me back, I think, 'Hey, is it me or is it them?'"

"When was this?" I asked.

Gretchen said, "Well, it was dark, so I'm thinking last night."

I had no idea I'd called her. "I don't think so," I said.

Gretchen said, "I'm coming over there."

"No...Maybe later ..."

"You got till twelve," she said.

High noon. Sounded reasonable, or at least something I couldn't stop. I dropped the phone on the floor and sank my face into the pillow again.

The next morning, or sometime thereabouts, the voice of my friend Ali, along with those of Alex and Caroline, wafted in from the hallway just outside the bedroom.

"Let's go, we have to bake," said Ali.

I thought, *God, let her be talking to anyone else but me.*

She wasn't.

Ali came into the room. "Cookies. School. No refusal option," she said as she yanked the twisted covers off of me. "We can start with oatmeal or chocolate chip, But, we will be starting with one of them. Now."

I didn't move. Baking meant a hot oven. Mixing. Plopping dough on a baking sheet. Baking meant standing.

"I don't think so," I said, trying to will the sheets piled on the floor back over my body.

To this day I don't know how she managed it, But, Ali had me in the last place I wanted to be: on my feet, and moving. Toward the kitchen, with its bowls, flour, sugar, eggs… and ketchup. As I taxied into the kitchen, Ali called Gretchen, as if this were any of her business.

I baked. For as long as I was being watched, I baked. But, just as no man is an island, no kitchen is a bathroom. And when Ali went for the Ladies, I bolted back to bed.

Exactly where I need to be, thought the newly minted shut-in, my safe place. The depressed—in every sense of the word—shell of the currently nonexistent Catherine Graves had to be exactly here.

Though my body felt more dead than alive, my senses hadn't been completely shorted out. I could hear Ali talking on the phone, probably assuming I was fully zonked, offering detail and opinion on whether and how much I'd eaten, if I'd showered, combed my hair, brushed my teeth. If it weren't so pathetic, it would have sounded like a parent calling a child at summer camp to see that she'd been keeping up on the activities that put us a quarter-rung higher on the evolutionary scale than chimps. But, as my sluggish central-processing unit whirred, I knew she was talking about me. To whom, I didn't know. Turned out it wasn't just a friend-to-friend daily update. She was talking to my therapist, Sarah, and Sarah was not at all amused by what she'd just heard. I suppose I should have been ready for that, but anticipating anything except my next turn at bat in the weeping league (which was now, thanks to Ali, overdue) was of no interest and probably impossible.

Ali held out the phone. I knew that not taking it would have more repercussions and leave me fewer options than accepting it. So I was linked up to Sarah, who proceeded to ask me a set of basic questions (What time is it? What day is it?). I couldn't talk, I couldn't speak. All I could do was cry.

Sarah listened to the labored vocalizations seeping out of me, then said, "I want you to go get some help. Do you remember what we talked about? It's time. It's way past time."

I did manage to utter a coherent single syllable. "Can't."

"You are severely depressed, Catherine. This isn't a topic for debate. You're not functioning well as a living human being. You need more help than I am able to give you at this time."

Somehow I found a way to defend myself, the worst lawyer in the world. "Well, I'm having a bad day. But I'm not having a nervous breakdown."

Sarah said, "Call it anything you want. But you're not having a bad day. From what I've heard, this is day number five. I'm leaving town and feel that it would be best for you to get some treatment outside of your home."

An indelible formula was chalked on the blackboard in my mind: Nervous breakdown = thirty-five days with no children, no phone, no contact to the outside world. As far as I was concerned I was not going to spend more than a month locked down in some treatment center that I never wanted to go to in the first place, and just because I was inconsolable and didn't want to bake cookies. I had every right to that much, didn't I?

Apparently not.

I thought, *Are you nuts?* I said, "I just can't do that."

I knew it was way expensive, and in my mind it wasn't worth it. I knew the kids wouldn't be joining me on what was going to be a useless psychological safari. They'd be out here, in the world, where they needed me. Alex and Caroline are great, But, a high schooler and an eighth-grader are not that well equipped to handle the complexities of the real world, no matter how smart or confident. Forget the fact that I couldn't handle the complexities of the world outside of my bedroom.

I handed the phone back to Ali, and went diver-down into the bed once more.

Sometime later—an hour or three, maybe a day—I came back up. But, I barely had the ability to resurface this time. I was wiped. I noticed the kids in the room, and they noticed the shape I was in. They brought me water. I don't think I could have gone to the well myself. I drained the glass. I let the empty glass drop on the bed. Then I noticed the babysitter, Stacy, who had been helping me with Alex and Caroline during John's ordeal, standing in the doorway of my bedroom.

She had been called in by Alex and Caroline. She had a sad, sympathetic smile on her face. I felt so embarrassed for her to see me this way, and incompetent for being weak in front of my children. She seemed compassionate and obviously concerned that I had gotten myself to this place.

One of my children -I can't quite recall which one (because it's too painful) - spoke up on behalf of the two of them. "You have to go to that place, Mom. The one Sarah was talking to you about."

Shaking my head, which only made me woozier than I already was, I said, "I can't leave you guys. You need me."

Now I am able to think back on that moment and shake my head: They needed who? At the time, I was some *place*. I may have been there in body, but, I sure as heck wasn't there with them in mind.

Alex said, "The other one Sarah talked to you about."

I held up my hand for a second, feeling nauseous. That was one of the last things I ever wanted to hear coming from my children. I didn't want them to know. I didn't want them to think about this. But how could they not?

Caroline added, "It's only for a week, Mom."

Still, I was as adamant as I could be. "That's too long. You guys can't be here by yourselves. No way," I said, again making the vertiginous mistake of shaking my head.

"Stacy'll be with us," Alex said. "She's stayed with us before."

Stacy took her cue and nodded her head. "It's not a big deal at all, Catherine. Really. I talked to Sarah. I'll be here the whole week. She's good with that, and so are the kids."

Like some cartoon character, all I could hear echoing in my head was, "No, I can't go, I can't go, I can't go."
Until Caroline broke that endless tape loop with a simple but, moving, "Please, Mom…"

Alex nodded. "It's got to be better than this. You know that too." Then he paused for a second as he looked me in the eyes. My handsome son, beautiful face marked by doubt and concern. "Right?"

My heart started to beat again, a little bit. The moment left me weak and I fell back on the bed. But I managed a weak, "OK." And suddenly my kids looked relieved and thankful that I had finally conceded. This time I cried a little for all the right reasons, and I said, "OK" one more time as the only gift I could give them at that moment.

"Nervous Breakdown"

As mysterious and elusive as a plaid unicorn, a reverse parallel universe the size of a dust mote. The nervous breakdown does not exist (I'm not sure about that universe, though). Not as an actual diagnosis of a human psychological condition, at least. Nervous breakdown, in layman's parlance, has its roots in the many-centuries-old concept of melancholia (as the word suggests, a form of persistent and resistant melancholy), and usually refers to a collection of disharmonic symptoms that come on simultaneously, almost always in response to an external trauma.

What people refer to as a "nervous breakdown" has all the hallmarks of a major depressive episode, along with symptoms of significant anxiety and a general inability for a person to accomplish everyday functions thrown in for bad measure. The only relatively (and I mean relatively) benign characteristic of a nervous breakdown is that it is generally of limited duration. The classic bundle of symptoms begins to diminish when the cause or causes of the emotional distress go away or diffuse with the inevitable passage, and sometimes kindness of time.

There is no one underlying cause of a nervous breakdown. Death, divorce, financial problems, career issues, problems at school, can all lead to this paralyzing behavior. (Stack any of them on top of each other, and you might have a *NERVOUS BREAKDOWN*. The closest hard diagnosis matching a nervous breakdown is referred to as an adjustment disorder with anxiety and transient depression. You may as well refer to it as an emotional tsunami for the way it comes on, rising up from what on the surface may seem a very calm sea.

The stress can build for a long time before you become close to temporarily dysfunctional. But when the syndrome or breakdown begins, fatigue, confusion, and hopelessness follow hard. You can't do anything. You don't want to do anything. You don't want anyone to do anything for you. It can be devastating, even if intellectually you know this is probably a temporary state of being.

Unlike true grief or bereavement, this is something that needs to be addressed as soon as possible. Mustering the necessary energy to seek a solution, though, can be seriously problematic, and this is where a friend, a relative, anyone who knows you, can step in and be a prime mover. It's where you can be of greatest assistance to a friend going through a crisis.

A nervous breakdown doesn't provide any catharsis. It is a serious-enough psychological low point that, though usually not life-threatening, needs intervention.

When you are experiencing it, you will not believe anything will stop the feelings you're having. It might be inconceivable to you to cross a room, much less cross a threshold to seek help. But you have to. Grief is brutal enough. A "breakdown," though it may precede, follow, or come in the middle of the grieving cycle, isn't something that should be tolerated. Don't let it run roughshod over you. Get help. Talk to a friend. Seek out a doctor. A group. Get the message out from your lips to their ears that you're in trouble. Don't be ashamed to ask. Shout it out, wave for help if you need to. But get it.

Paralysis does not equal healthy self-analysis. "Nervous breakdowns" are just debilitating. They freeze your brain, which freezes your life. And you're likely to have more than enough real-life issues to deal with after such an episode that you do yourself no favors by dwelling in the Breakdown Lane for a second longer than necessary.

12.

"Hi, my name's Catherine, and I'm a grief-aholic ..."

No, not that. Not quite that. Not even close to that. But that's what it felt like when I first presented myself to the group I'd be working with at Psychological Counseling Services in Scottsdale. I still didn't think I belonged in this place, didn't feel what I'd been going through deserved this much attention. There were people I was sitting with, sitting right next to me, who were telling stories of sexual abuse, near-psychotic episodes caused by pressures I couldn't even imagine being part of my life. I had to tell my story. Tell the truth, tell it straight. Suddenly I felt that my story would be too common, too insignificant to even mention. I mean, death is as much a part of life as life itself, isn't it? I remember hearing the gruesome old statistic that there are far more dead people on earth than there were (or are) living at any one time. So I couldn't have expected that anyone-- John, me, my family, anyone I love, or even didn't particularly like-- would live forever. We all come to the same end. Why couldn't I just accept it?

Because circumstance and context means everything. I'd learn this later. I probably sensed it now, but I couldn't put it into words, nor could I put that nascent knowledge into action. So here I was, about to tell a group of strangers about the Tragedy of Catherine the Graves.

"My husband died eighteen months ago. Then my step-mother passed away. And my dog just died."

This was not a country and western song. This had been my life over the past year and a half. But reduced to those three little speaking points, even to me it didn't sound like a heck of a lot. What were these people going to think? Was I about to be voted off the island?

I waited. They waited, expecting more. Where was the real bad stuff?

I didn't have any more. Not at the moment, at least. Not the way I saw it.

The silence was finally broken when someone spoke up: "Could you not... um... smile when you tell us, and tell us again?"

There are times when you feel like The Great Unwanted Spotlight is on you and you've just recited a Wanda Sykes routine instead of the expected Hamlet soliloquy. This was one of those times multiplied.

So I said what I'd already said again, this time with molars locked down, lips stiff as a mannequin.

I waited. That was what they had wanted. I thought.

Not quite.

"Uh, could you tell us again? But, slow it down."

OK, I said to myself, that was valid. I knew this was not a contest. The Fastest Tragic Teller of Tales would not be carrying home a trophy and cash prizes.

I went through my short, miserable tale one more time, unsmiling, under the speed limit, and then I clamped down. The group was either satisfied or they couldn't bear to hear another not-quite-perfect variant of the same three facts, and so we moved on.

I couldn't have felt less connected to this process if someone had actually physically pulled my plug out of the wall socket. Twelve hours a day of this for the next week. Me thinking, *I am in a public-speaking class that I don't need to graduate from. I may have to slip silently out of this room, and not haunt these halls again.*

First impressions, though, are never always right, I don't care what anyone says. And my first impression of this place and this group was off center by about half a world. So I sat in my spot, uneasily waiting the next exercise, anticipating disaster, and unable to hope for much more than that.

It may not seem like much, but that's all I remember from my first day of Healing Thyself 101. There were individual sessions, group sessions and more sessions. Just another day at your local mental hospital.

I do remember that someone pointed out that I was maybe, well…too upbeat for someone who was in for a week's worth of intensive therapy. I told them I'd always been optimistic. Of course, I didn't tell them of the five lost days in my bedroom. The weeks of despair before and after John was diagnosed. The exhausting emotional roller-coaster of his treatments, and ultimately of his last days. To me, that was not getting-to-know-you chatter.

Even though I felt I'd kind of skated through the first day at PCS, I was blown away when I went back to the Royal Palms, where I was staying for the week. It was a beautiful hotel, away from the reminders I didn't need to be reminded of, and the real and imagined stresses at home. At that point I thought, *maybe this was all I needed. A week in beautiful surroundings without any significant cares.* Sure, it was delusional. But I was in no condition to judge that. I was trying to be Catherine Graves, Survivor Extraordinaire, not Catherine Graves, a Woman in Trouble.

I crashed in the big bed. But I was determined not to get stuck there. This bed would not hold an imprint of my body. I'd get up and out every day. I was determined to get better. But I was going to have to work at it, that much I knew. All

I had to do was think of the faces of my Alex and Caroline. For them I'd shove the world out of orbit.

13.

Living a life that turns into a tale worth telling is not always a blessing. Everyone's life is its own story, writ large or small, depending on the personality of the author. Some don't need or want their stories told. And that's fine. I was one of those people a lifetime ago. I didn't want to live a life worth a book or a magazine piece, nor even a short prize-winning film with the part of me being played by Sandra Bullock. I craved a normal life with a husband I'd spend a long time with that would be so wonderful that, fifty years later, it would feel like only a moment had passed. I wanted us to raise our children, watch them grow and flourish, and not worry ourselves to death or their distraction over the increasingly complex world they'd have to face.

But I realize now that if you want to get into the habit of predicting the ultimate course of your life, you may as well be in the business of predicting the precise shape of the next cloud that will pass over the furthest mountain you can see—and the exact moment it happens. My life did not follow that path I'd so desired. And it did become, I think, a story worth telling, illustrating the unpredictability of life and being able to offer some hard-earned, well-polished gems of advice on how to negotiate the road *after* you've been through the unseen, terrifying hairpin turn.

The first place I told my story was of course at PCS, and that first, befuddled day was just the beginning of my healing process. We worked with psychodrama (officially defined as "a psychotherapeutic technique in which people are assigned roles to be played spontaneously within a dramatic context devised by a therapist in order to understand the behavior of people with whom they have difficult interactions"). I defined the process on my own terms, breaking the word into two and applying each half to me at different times of my life, psycho...and drama. Eye Movement Desensitization and Reprocessing (EMDR)—more on this later, I promise. And group therapy, during which I told all the details that had led me to the conclusion that John had been having an affair. After I spoke for what seemed to me an hour, but was probably more on the order of five and a half minutes, one of the other members of the group spoke up.

"So he ... wasn't having an affair?"

"No," I answered.

"Never?"

I shook my head. "Not even close." I could feel a little disappointment in the room, as if I'd detailed an astonishing tale of hunting an escaped lion in the suburbs of Phoenix, only to reveal at the end that there was no lion and I'd never actually left my living room.

Everyone began exchanging stories, comparing notes on their personal experiences when they suspected their partners of having infidelities. Although I still felt that the affair I'd imagined John was having ultimately had more tragic results than the others in the room, who was I to judge? I didn't know what these betrayals had done to this group of fragile strangers.

Move on to the next person, I said quietly to myself. *Move on.*

No such luck.

Our group counselor turned to me and asked, "What else was going on in your life at the time? Other problems? Other distractions?"

I explained to them that I was running a business with the man I loved who was not supposed to be a silent partner, but who became utterly uninvolved, even when I pointed out to him that, though we were busy, the business was inexplicably sort of broke.

I continued to say that when I found out one of our foremen had been taking cash payments upfront from customers and gambling it away, I asked John if he was going to fire him or was he going to make me do it.

John's response: "Why fire him at all?"

My next thought: Maybe John was in on the game.

So I guess you could say I had some righteously serious, non-imaginary business concerns that weighed about sixteen tons, and were too heavy a load to me to carry.
Someone in group asked, "So did your husband have a gambling addiction?"

I bit my lip a little. I knew where this going. "No."

A small disappointed "Oh" escaped her lips.

Then, I suppose just for confirmation's sake, another member of the group said, "And he wasn't really having an affair?"

Shook my head. I think that was all that was needed.

But then came the oddest sentence one could ever think of coming to one's rescue: "Well, how did he die?"

I looked up. I could tell this story. I had many times before, and I needed to keep telling it so that I could ultimately understand and believe it..

The group was back with me, and though I would be telling them an awful story, they'd all shared tough stories of their own lives. Unlike Groucho Marx, I did care to belong to a club that would accept someone like me as a member.

Not forever, mind you. But for now I wanted it more than just about anything.

EMDR, or What You See Is What You Saw

Eye Movement Desensitization and Reprocessing therapy hasn't been around that long, at least not compared with the traditional tools (talk, cognitive, pharmaceutical therapies) in the psychiatric medical bag. It was developed in the early 1990s by psychiatrist Francine Shapiro. Though controversial at first, the evidence that it is significantly beneficial to people who have lived through traumatic events, particularly patients suffering from post traumatic stress disease, is compelling enough to have been accepted by the larger psychiatric community. I could explain in my own terms how it works, but it's a technically unwieldy subject, with various types of equipment employed, and different treatment steps for different types of trauma and disorders, so I'm not going to. Plus, it would almost sound like something I'd made up. Here's a concise, dead accurate description from the EMDR-Therapy Web site:

"...EMDR therapy uses bilateral stimulation, right/left eye movement, or tactile stimulation, which repeatedly activates the opposite sides of the brain, releasing emotional experiences that are 'trapped' in the nervous system. This assists the neurophysiological system, the basis of the mind/body connection, to free itself of blockages and reconnect itself.

As troubling images and feelings are processed by the brain via the eye-movement patterns of EMDR, resolution of the issues and a more peaceful state are achieved."

So there.

For the practical purposes of my therapy, what it came down to was me wearing a headset and holding vibrating sensors in my hand while my counselor guided me through my narrative of difficult emotional memories. The sounds and vibrations I experienced from the equipment during these sessions would enable me to confront these issues in a new way, from a new direction. See them, literally and figuratively, in a new light, and file them in a part of my brain where I could cope with them in a panic-less state and have more of a sense of proportional reality of what I'd gone through.

In short, it would help me come to the realization that I could tolerate the memories of the terrible events of John's illness and death and live through them. That's no small thing.

Some medical professionals have been trying to debunk EMDR since it was first introduced, but they've met with little or no success. (Luckily for me and thousands of others who have been successfully treated with EMDR.) In fact this form of therapy is used by the Armed Services for soldiers returning from the battlefield with PTSD, and with everyday citizens dealing with panic, obsessive-compulsive, dissociative, and dysmorphic body disorders, as well as "… depression, grief, addictions, eating disorders, body image disturbances, issues of self-esteem, morbid jealousy, chronic pain, test anxiety, personality disorders, public-speaking anxiety, somatoform disorders, substance abuse, and some aspects of Attention-Deficit/Hyperactivity Disorder as well." (This from *Traumatology*, Vol. 9, No. 3, in an article authored by Charlotte Sikes and Victoria Sikes.)

It is not the be all and end all for every psychiatric illness. The bottom line, though, is that while aspects of the therapy, including light flashes, odd sounds, and vibrations, may seem quite odd to the majority of people who have never experienced it, EMDR is as effective as cognitive behavior therapy and medication for particular kinds of psychiatric illness and trauma.

The distress one has experienced becomes "unstuck" from your mind; you no longer skip to it immediately and allow it to color and control your every thought, as one frequently does after a devastating occurrence. The therapy helps a patient to place trauma it in its proper place, its correct context, in the long story of one's life.

You don't do EMDR year after year after year, as some people do with talk and/or medication therapy. And its positive effects frequently last as long, or longer, as those of more conventional cognitive therapies.

I have no doubt that it helped move me down the road back to my life. If you think it might help you, there's enough information on the Web and in books to get you comfortable with the idea and help you find the right practitioner for you. Don't be afraid or embarrassed to try it. It's not physically painful, though it can be mentally draining for a while. But odds are you'll be able to think straight again, maybe for the first time since a significant traumatic event overcame you. And how many things in your life can you say might help you get to that absolutely necessary point in healing?

14.

"Do you feel alone?" The person asking the question was me. The person in our group I was addressing also happened to be me, and I was by myself, so lying would serve no purpose. I was nearly at the end of my weeklong therapy workout at PCS, and though I'd been a little dubious, somewhat apprehensive, at first, I'd found a path I wouldn't have otherwise stumbled on to the truth of how I'd been living and what I'd actually been feeling. So, did I feel alone?

You bet. And though I now understood my feelings of isolation, it didn't mean I was equipped yet to handle those feelings in the great wide world outside the walls of PCS, or my hotel room.

The night before my last day at PCS I called Alex and Caroline to talk to them about possibly extending my stay. I had to tell them truthfully how I was doing. "I'm ... you know ... OK. Pretty steady," I said in an unsteady voice loaded with unokayness.

When one person out of three finds an answer unacceptable, you can usually ignore it. When three out of three know the answer you've just given isn't quite good enough, it offers its own ready-made conclusion.

It was the right thing to do. We all knew it. They didn't want to see me crawl into the Twilight Zone of my bed again, and I couldn't bear doing that to them. Or, frankly, to myself. You have to maintain some sense of self-preservation in everything you do. No one can do that for you. None of us had to like the decision, and there wasn't any discussion. It just felt like the right thing to do, and we were all in agreement.

Week Two (or as I thought of it, Weak Too) was exhausting, draining, dehydrating.

Heavy on the EMDR, it seemed. Light, sound, vibrations. But it all seemed to weigh so heavily on the imaginary measuring scale I weighed my life on. Twelve-hour daily sessions, just like the week before, but now I wrung out every day, dry-cleaned it and hung it up for the night in a cheap plastic bag. But I began to believe that this discomfort was a good thing. Being exhausted with sharing my story, getting tired of my own self, meant I was beginning to accept the things that had happened to John, to me, to the kids as an undeniable truth. Something I would eventually learn to live with, with a minimum, but never the complete absence, of pain. I was beginning to accept loss as an inevitable but survivable aspect of life. It sounds like such a simple thing now; it may just be the understanding of this concept that makes human beings what we are. I don't know. I don't want to be the one to write the definitive Rulebook for Being Human but this was a moment when I knew I could return home to my kids, our home, our lives. We could build our futures on our experiences, no matter how unsettling, rather than fearing them, shunning then, and allowing it to eat away at any new foundation we could establish.

True, I did end in up one of my final sessions doubled up, weeping as if I would never be able to stop. The realization of the loss I had endured had finally begun to expose itself, allowing me to remember not only the treacherous, miserable, lonely sad times but the joyous, gratifying, and loving times that we shared together. Those times were just beginning to surface, and have continued to be ongoing in my memory. But I think I needed a great big catharsis to get me out the door and back on the road and into the world I belonged in.

I was as ready as I'd ever be to head home.

At least in theory. Just before I said my final farewells, auf wiedersehens, adieus, I thought, possibly out loud that I could use just one more week. I'd come so far over the past two weeks that I knew a third week, just one little third week would set everything I'd learned in fourteen days—

about myself, my past, my life, my emotions, coping measures, meditative moments, alone and together time—in concrete. I needed just seven more days to add a little reinforcement.

It was probably my worst instinct of my treatment at PCS, and luckily everyone who worked there, everyone I therapied with there, knew it as well. Before I left, though, I made a little list of some things I'd learned. Among the items on that inventory were: "I've learned about unconditional love," "I have learned about forgiveness," "I have learned not to lean so heavily on the phrase 'I don't know,'" and, possibly most importantly, "I have found my true voice."

I was not thrown out of the front door to land on my rump with a comical thump like some cartoon character, though I may have deserved it. I was led graciously through the exit process, accompanied to the front door, then a short walk to my car, and I was off again in the real world.

Hey, I thought, *I've been here before.* Everything looked familiar, though somehow now it all looked a bit clearer. Yes, I knew I was home, But not yet Home, and when I pulled into the driveway, created with the paving stones that John and I sold, I knew that a third week at PCS would have been a little helpful, but probably self-indulgent, and absolutely the wrong thing to do. This is where I needed to be. At the house I shared with my children and a million memories of John. Memories I knew I could acknowledge and accept.

I had my foundation: now I had some serious rebuilding to do. Deep plates of an earthquaked life to maneuver back into place so the earth no longer seemed to shake under our feet. I had to hold it together.There was a lot of love here. There was nothing that could destroy our family. But, no matter what age or how intelligent your child is, there's bound to be the slightest bit of resentment for my having been away and pulling myself together again.

I hadn't achieved the perfect level of understanding, but Alex and Caroline had lived through the same trauma, albeit in different roles, different maturity levels and with very different relationships with John. But they'd soldiered on, through school, through sports, homework, their complex and unknowable after-school lives. I think, in their eyes, I'd sort of flaked on them. I knew I needed them back. They were, and remain, the foundation of my life. And they knew they needed me. But there was a bit of trepidation in their "welcome home" even though they'd been largely responsible for my proper decision to go to PCS.

Make no mistake. They were as thrilled to have me home as I was to be there. But, I needed to prove myself to them. And they had every right to expect that of me. So I set out to do exactly that. But one small matter to tend to first…

I had to close down the business immediately, with "immediately" defined as months ago. The recession had hit Phoenix even harder than most places, and the real-estate and new-home segment of the local economy was somewhere near the Titanic. I was down to three employees (three lovely women without whom things would have fallen into absolute chaos long before this), and they knew as well as I did that the brakes had to be slammed on. So, that's what I did. I slammed on the brakes.

My father, David, came down from my hometown of St. Louis to help me with the huge unwieldy pile of complexities that a fading business becomes. It took a month and a half of negotiations, renegotiations, sell-offs, auctions, giveaways, and papers to sign and sign and sign. By the end of the process, a lifetime spent back at PCS seemed like an awfully comforting idea. But instead, I had become Catherine, The Businesswoman with at least a lick of sense, and Villa Pavers was soon to be just a memory.

It was not an enjoyable process, believe me. My three employees had to head into the great unemployment storm to find new work. The business I had started and worked diligently with John (before the first signs of his illness) to nourish and develop was now history. It was the right thing to do. The only thing to do. But it was costly and painful, like yanking off a full-body Band-Aid. I try not to think about it too often, but when I do, I think about John and me in the early, we-can-accomplish-anything days of the business, and I now can smile a little at that memory.

But luckily I didn't have time to reminisce about things, business or pleasure. Instead, I had the most important business of my life at hand—reconnecting with Alex and

Caroline. I could not allow that emotional motor to stop turning. You lose your kids, you lose your world. It really is that simple. There is nothing ahead of you, and the things behind me were not what I wanted to spend the rest of my life dwelling on.

I might have driven the kids a little crazy, but teenagers are a little crazy anyway, so I don't think my attentions were adding too much more angst to the mix. Once I had finished working on myself at PCS—what I'd become to think of as my Emotional Finishing School—I believe I became a better, more attentive, more sensitive mother. You'll have to ask Alex and Caroline, but I don't think I'm breaking my arm to pat myself on the back here.

We took trips together, just the three of us. Something I never before thought I'd be able to plan and perform on my own without asking someone or everyone I knew a thousand questions: how, which, why, where, who, when, and 994 more just like those. But I didn't do that. I arranged the trips myself. My lovely, wonderful children and I traveled together to see friends, to see sights we'd never seen. We talked the whole time, and filled our heads with new sounds and visions. A unified family vision. Our minds didn't work in lockstep (not with three strong-willed people, no matter how pleasing the circumstances). But we did finally become…restful again. Comfortable with ourselves and with one another. Unafraid to express our thoughts because the stress of the moment might make that expression seem more loaded with some phantom significance.

We were a family again. With one member missing, still very much loved and alive in our thoughts and memories. But we all knew that dwelling on the past two years, chewing on it like a piece of leather that just won't be chewed down, served no purpose. That's where bitterness comes from, and we did not need that flavor in our lives.

We still live in our house. The house John and I bought and remodeled together after we married. And it feels right to be here. It is not discomforting, something I'd feared, to be in a place where the great good and the very bad stuff of life has occurred. If anything, it can keep you grounded. You know that life is a heck of a lot more complicated than a box of chocolates. Alex and Caroline are in school. They're doing great, and doing everything fine, not so fine, and everything in between that people their ages are supposed to do—and not.

And though I can't quite believe it myself, for a while there I volunteered at Barrows Neurological Institute, where John was treated and where I fought a lot of hard emotional battles, inside and out. I didn't tell the families there my story. If they ever know it, they'll know it from reading it here. They were going through their own crises and struggles. I tried to steer them through the hard times, the complications, give bits of advice when they asked for it, but I didn't reveal the source of what I hoped seemed like wisdom to them. It was hard won, and at Barrows I liked to keep John's story to myself. I let it inform my actions, and put it to the best use I knew how.

There is an odd sense of freedom—from the past, from misplaced guilt, from dwelling too long on things that were too hard—in helping these people. In most cases, they're going through many of the same emotions I never imagined I'd go through when John's incomprehensible symptoms first began to appear at the beginning of that long tragic journey.

But unlike the great song lyric by Kris Kristofferson, I don't think freedom is just another word for nothing left to lose. For me, freedom is finally coming to the understanding that it is impossible to lose everything unless you lose yourself.

Part Three
The 14,596 Mishaps, Lessons, and Wisdom I Made, Learned, and Gained, Fully Illustrated

15.

Admission: I stumbled and misstepped through an emotional, physical, and psychological minefield—much of which was not my creation, some of which I worked extra hard to lovingly craft myself—of such devastating complexity, I couldn't recreate it if I tried. Looking back, I feel that I learned simple lessons about things I already might have known and unexpected lessons about matters I never wanted to imagine. I gained, if not formal wisdom, at least a kind of survivor's sixth sense. I can't say I need to impart these insights to you, or that you necessarily need me to. That's too tall an order for a humble, new writer to take on. But those of you who have read this story might be interested in how I was finally able to pick out the mistakes threaded through the big rug of my life and what I might have done not to weave them in to that beautiful tapestry. You might recognize yourself in my mirror, gazing, and step back from a brink that I happily am no longer on.

I couldn't have predicted, controlled, or even avoided the things that happened to me or the things I brought on myself. Perhaps I could have, if I had been rational, calm, levelheaded, and not watching the man I loved disappear in front of me. But that wasn't the case. I feel that I just went ahead, though, accepting and becoming a willing participant in actions that did me wrong as if they were inevitable. I deluded myself that either they weren't actually happening or that they weren't having any ultimately incapacitating effects. I lost my objectivity, the clearheaded point of view that had always gotten me through tough times.

Now I'm back to Square One, which is where I want to be. I have a clear enough view of my life that when things seem to be going wrong, I trust my first, natural instincts. And, as I'd done for most of my life, I know I can make a plan for slowing things down or stopping something right in its tracks.

I think—OK, I know—I made the oldest mistake in the book. I assumed that I knew everything about what was going on around me, and that I should have the answers for everything. It's horrible that it's true, but when you assume, you do make an *ass* of *u* and *me*. In this case, mostly me.

I couldn't have known everything there was to know. I was a woman in deep distress. I am not a super woman, I am just a person. I make mistakes. All of the decisions were up to me and mine to make. Lord knows I tried my best to carefully consider all the information that was being shoved at me. But it really does come fast and furious in dire health-related situations. It's like trying to respond to lightning before it strikes.

In the big picture (which you don't see until the painting is all but done), the circumstances surrounding John's illness might have seemed to unfold slowly over time. But I was seeing so many conflicting and strange behaviors from him, and having to make so many decisions from mundane to lifesaving, I couldn't put together the jigsaw puzzle of what I was experiencing fast enough. It just wasn't possible. Sometimes you just can't get a clear perspective when you're smack in the middle.

I made a lot of wrong assumptions about the way John was behaving, culled from a list of the most obvious and most likely causes (philandering, drug abuse, and the possibility of his just having fallen out of love with me). I didn't know, couldn't have known, that John was having small, almost imperceptible, symptoms for a long time before his behavior started to get suspicious and uncharacteristic. But he couldn't know, anymore than I could have known that everyday events such as random headaches and an occasional pain between the eyes would come to be the beginning of the editable end. Who doesn't have headaches now and again? I've got friends who swear they have headaches everyday.

By the time those little miscues were firing off more regularly with John, his ability to think straight was already starting to fail. The chance of him deciding to seek out serious medical attention for them, or even bothering to mention them to me, was nonexistent. Sure, I was with John when some of these "symptoms" occurred, but it wasn't until much later that I even realized that they were the first signs of something much bigger than we imagined.

As I look back, I wish I could say that I documented, kept some kind of a list of the things I was seeing that would have added up to John's getting treatment earlier. (Of course, the nature of his illness made that a moot point.) Sometimes I can't sleep, wondering if there was more that I could have done. The plain truth is that I couldn't. If John's disease had been something different, with symptoms that spelled out in large letters that Something Significant Is Wrong Here, sure, I could have done something. But there was no pattern to see in John's case, no neon signs. I don't, I can't, hold myself responsible for missing something obvious. Because everything he was experiencing in the beginning was too everyday and matter of fact. Eternal vigilance would have burned me out, and I still wouldn't have seen the truth behind what I was seeing on the surface of our lives. No one can. I punished myself for a long time for not being able to do, if not the impossible, at least the improbable. No one should be that hard on herself.

To say that I was shocked by the reality of John's ultimate diagnosis would be the greatest understatement of my life. If any of the things I initially suspected about John had been true (the now obviously petty things), I would have been profoundly upset, discombobulated, let down, miffed (to say the least). If what actually came to pass was something I could have correctly predicted from the information I'd gathered, I surely would have done so.

My ability (or lack thereof) to play catch up when the tragic conditions in my life were progressing at light speed had nothing to do with my natural abilities or insensitivities. Circumstance is like water: it goes wherever it wants and will always find a way in, no matter what. It doesn't have emotions or a conscious. Circumstance just is. The jolt and subsequent aftershocks from misfortune I was receiving were absolutely paralyzing. I couldn't move ahead of that wave. I was inundated by it and it tsunamied through the lives of the people I loved the most.

I did keep myself informed as well as I could, and retained as much of the overdose of information I was receiving. That was the best I could do, and I have to give myself some credit for even being able to do that. I couldn't duck the big wave that smacked me from a direction I never even knew existed. And I sure couldn't dive under the bigger one that was hiding right behind it. The sheer power of that huge emotional wave wasn't something I could control. But I did try my best to stay ahead of it, even as it overtook and overpowered me. Being overwhelmed but, informed beats clueless paralysis every time. I was at least able to make some moves to protect myself, my kids, and do the best for John that I could by having some understanding of what we were facing.

Sure, still waters run deep. When John's rare situation came to the forefront of my life, the sheer volume of information, misinformation, intelligent and two-bit opinions, confusion and clarity, and ultimately actions, reactions, and inaction I faced was simply overpowering. Any step I took needed much more deliberation than I could have possibly given it at the time. Tough and daunting decisions were thrown at me all at once. My patience, my discretion was in short supply. But, when I finally had the chance to take a quick look over my shoulder, I knew that having been able to consider those steps with clear, unfiltered focus would have saved a lot of personal pain for my family and me.

Not every decision I had to make was literally life or death. But some of them were. I needed to understand not only my own location and position, but also those occupied by John. They were very different, as you might imagine. What was best, most comforting, possibly an easier decision for me was not necessarily the best decision for him. I was on the edge of a precarious emotional path. I was able to see that if the choice I made in some cases for John would leave me in a far worse and kind of wrecked position. No matter how selfless I wanted to be, it was still a complex process to go through, to understand just how deep and fast the water was that I could survive.

Ultimately, I realize that making the choice that benefitted John (or in some cases, the kids) was always the right decision. Sometimes I was lucky and found that the choice was the one I wanted to make anyway. Those situations sure made my everyday life during this chaotic time with John healthier, happier, and longer lasting. But we're all grown-ups here, right? We know that right decisions don't always lead to happy endings. Right decisions can leave you absolutely devastated, as they did me.

It's also a time when I felt lost in the woods for a while. That's when I needed my network of friends, family, even strangers who may have gone through the same things standing ready to lend support. I know now that if someone—even some stranger nearby—has a brutal decision to make, it will only be right to sacrifice something significant of myself for their sake. There are depths that take a long time and an enormous amount of effort to rise from, and as I found from rough experience there was no advantage in letting myself drift that far down. When my internal navigation was temporarily trashed, my friends needed to step in, steady me, and lift me back up. Only then could I take a deep breath. See how sweet the air was. What I was tasting there was my life. I breathed it in, and eventually found that it was all the sustenance I needed.

One thing I needed to develop, though I didn't know it at the time, was a built-in warning system against making ill-advised (i.e., really, really dumb) decisions when I was at a point of extreme exhaustion and grief. It was a hard lesson for me to learn. When I was completely played out, disoriented, throat parched, I should have had the ability to decide to have a great big tumbler of cool water. If I decided instead to have a great big tumbler of vodka taken straight from a bottle in the freezer, my early warning system would have gone off and stopped my hand in midair.

My decision-making skills ebbed and flowed like the Mississippi River. My senses of self-regard, self-respect, self-esteem, self-protection were absolutely nonexistent for a time. I believe I was subconsciously displaying an unhealthy façade of self-destruction. It was largely invisible to me, but was blindingly obvious to friends and predators alike.

Caroline: *If I were to have to give advice to anyone my age going through this, I would say hang in there. It's the hardest thing ever. Especially when you're young. John was my dad. I don't mean that as an insult to my real dad. But I spent all my time with John, he raised me. I don't feel like my "stepdad" died, I feel like my dad died.*

John passed away when I was twelve years old. If anyone goes through what I went through, I'd tell them to stay close to your friends and family. They'll all help you get through it. Don't cut yourself off from the whole world. You may need time and isolation, but not forever.

Create memories. More than you already have. You'll want to look back on the great things that you did with the person you loved. I, unlike most people, only remember some things, the weird ones. I like it though. I can remember the hard things if they are triggered, but unless they are, I remember the good, the funny and the goofy.

Write! I wrote a lot. I used to have a MySpace page, and one way that helped me feel better was writing a little dedication sort of thing to John in my "heroes" section on my profile. I was always changing it. And I used to save each one that I wrote.

I also sometimes wrote little letters, and then deleted them. But writing about how I was feeling really helped. Some things in life are hard when they happen, then even harder to get through. But in the end, things will be OK.

John is with me every day. He is by my side through everything that I do. He made it so that I remember the good things instead of the bad. He created those memories for me so that now I can look back on them and smile.

Alex: *There's nothing I can say that would make someone's pain go away. I would never say something to give a person false hope, something that tries to make anyone feel better that just isn't true. There is nothing that will help. You just have to step up, think about the good times, and never forget them. Never forget what* *the person you love believed, what they represented, and who they were. Things will get better though, I promise that.*

I got to the point where I didn't want to listen to advice from friends; I was sick to death of it. (Even though I'm sure I was subconsciously begging for guidance all along.) I did not pay attention to my own internal warning system: I didn't turn away from danger and in the direction of people I trusted for their points of view. But amazingly, I did not lose anyone as a result of my lack of patience. I was luckier than I deserved to be. It would have been a good idea for me to spend some time alone with my thoughts and myself, even though they were the last things I wanted to be alone with. My thoughts weren't truly melancholic or self-destructive. They were borne of exhaustion and of the dynamics of the situation. If I felt that I was truly depressed, I would have sought help immediately, as anyone should. That's dangerous stuff not even I would have been too deluded to think I could play with.

I wanted to grab hold of a friend near and dear when I was about to do something I knew would be…let's be kind and say ill-advised, and say, "Do not let me do this. I am giving you the power to stop me from jumping into any stupid decision, action, or relationship. I may try to argue with you unto death about what or whom I think I need or want. Don't listen to me. I won't know what I'm talking about." It's not that easy to ask for this, and I didn't. I didn't want to seem a burden. I didn't want to be seen as weak, unable to make coherent decisions. I wanted to appear that I could take care of myself.

I know enough not to worry about that stuff now.

I know it takes time for a troubled mind to settle. So much isn't understood about how the brain works, how the mix of chemicals and the mechanics of the brain change and interact during times of stress, despair, crushing responsibility, guilt, and self-doubt. I found myself facing an unfathomable personal loss. I was bound to make a bad choice now and again. I wasn't right in the head for a bit. Confusion really did reign supreme during and after overwhelming times, and I needed to concentrate on simple things— breathing, placing one foot in front of the other, trying to forgive lasagna (though this may never be possible.)

I was offered help, opinions, and interventions all the time. Sometimes I accepted. Other times, much to my everlasting humility, I did not. What resulted was one of the worst decisions I would make during my life after John. I survived it. I learned a hard lesson. I don't want anyone else to ever have to learn a lesson that demeaning.

My early warning system is now in place, and working. Sometimes I hit the test button to see what will happen. What happens is my friends come running. And I'm just lucky that way.

For a while I was stuck in reverse in my emotional transmission: I didn't have the desire to heal. A condition called survivor's guilt is real (which was, until the newly issued edition of Diagnostic and Statistical Manual the of Mental

Disorders, considered a syndrome apart from any other). My personal guilt trip—deserved or not—became an endless circle, a self-perpetuating drag. I found that I had to let myself run off the road, through the ditch, and into the long weeds before I could then slowly ease my way back toward the highway of life.

After John died, I began with routine tasks, small things that I once took for granted. I started to reconnect with friends I'd become disengaged from. I wasn't shooting 100 percent Me overnight. (The world, my world, any alternate world, probably couldn't take that.) But I carefully increased the content of my life until it began to feel like my own again.

Even at a relatively modest rate of acceleration, though, I made mistakes, chose the wrong door, angered and annoyed people now and again. But I avoided giant pitfalls. And the little screwups I was able to set right with the good graces and understanding of my friends and family. I even managed to pluck some lessons from things I'd mistakenly tossed into the discard pile. Probably the most important lesson being to allow myself to remember.

Memories can be paralyzingly painful. But they can also be remarkably energizing and inspiring. I began to recognize almost immediately when a particular memory was sending me into a deep funk, and I would put a halt on that thought. I'm not saying that I wanted to completely forget the hard times, but I had to know that what I'd just gone through was not typical of what my life had been nor would become.

In the future it will be important for me to recall the toughest of those times, and take a look at what it took for me to get through them. I need to do this for my own sake, and so I can one day offer help to someone else who seems on the hard edge of being devoured by a similar experience. There is a brutal significant value in surviving a grueling time but the time to reflect for me—I think for anyone—is when it is small in the rearview mirror, not when it still dominates the landscape.

So I did take a half-step back from what it would eventually take for me to heal completely. But it was an essential half-step back. Artists learn about the importance of perspective early on. Non-artists should take a lesson from that. When I learned to control the type and speed of memories that came back to me, I was able to accomplish what I wanted when I wanted it. I learned to refuse to cripple myself so that I wouldn't stand frozen as the great possibilities of my coming life passed me by.

ॐॐ

This seems like it shouldn't be that tough a thing to say: I didn't do anything wrong. At least not intentionally. It feels a bit embarrassing to express that, but if I stopped doing things that were potentially embarrassing, the only thing I'd ever do would be to brush my teeth and go back to bed.

Sometimes in those quiet moments, when I'm by myself, I take a look in the mirror and tell myself that I did the best I could by the people I loved, by the people who were depending on the choices I made, by anyone whose life was materially or spiritually changed by my decisions.

I wasn't the mayor of a town called Malice before the troubles presented themselves, and I know I didn't choose to take on that role in the midst of the process I had worked through. I know sincerely and definitively that the conclusions I came to were reached after serious thought and the consideration of all the information that was available to me at the time. They did not result in the miraculous outcome I was hoping for, but how often does that really happen in anyone's life?

Anyone I truly needed to apologize to has long since received that contrition. I remain true to those things I have always sincerely believed in-- the choices that I made, the people whom I love. I can embrace the hard times as well as the good. I know I never need to be ashamed and will never walk away from the wiser, kinder person I believe I've become from an astonishing and hard-fought journey.

Caroline: *John William Graves is my hero. I love him more than anything in the entire world. He is the strongest, funniest, nicest, world's-greatest Man of Steel the world will ever know.*

Catherine Graves is the strongest woman anyone will ever meet. She has gone through a whirlwind of bad events and has come out a completely changed person. I respect her so much, appreciate everything that she does for my brother and me, commend her for making it through what has happened, and love her to the moon and back for being the best mom I could ask for.

Alex: *John William Graves was the greatest man I have ever known. He was the funniest, nicest, compassionate human being that has ever walked the face of this earth and he will never be forgotten. Catherine Graves is one of the strongest women that I have ever seen. She has gone through more than anyone could ever be asked to go through. She's had some troubles, but has always seemed to come back even stronger afterwards, and I love her for it.*

Epilogue
The Dark Room
and the Man
With the Moon

The room is mine. The room is black. Solid, impenetrable black. I stand somewhere in it. Reach out with both hands, feel nothing, then a sense of vertigo, feeling as if I am standing in an infinite space with nothing familiar to touch, nothing to balance against.

I tentatively slide one foot forward. Bump into nothing, so edge the other ahead too. I know there are walls, objects. I call out and my voice does not just continue out into a void or echo against strange hard surfaces. It softly wraps around objects in the room, bounces between them and is then is absorbed by things I can't see.

I take a bold step forward and catch a sharp, hard edge across the shin for my courage. I feel my sudden surge of nerve flat-line then and there. I bend down, touch the wooden surface of a table, cautiously sit down on its edge to rest and center myself. The table collapses instantly under me, and I am on the floor.

I stand up fast from the broken wood and sharp straw blades and get dizzy as my heart lags behind, not pumping hard or fast enough to catch up with my head. It seems impossible to get my bearings, but I need some confidence before I take another step.

My hip comes to rest against the side of a chair. A big one. Upholstered, but with a fabric I don't recognize. I run my hand along the top, hoping for an easy tactile clue and am rewarded with an electric shock, more intense than could be accounted for with a simple static charge. I take a big step forward away from the chair, not caring what I might smack or tumble into. Nothing, so I stand in the black void again, which doesn't seem such a bad thing for the moment.

Frustrated that I should know this place but don't, I am exhausted, confused, and I know I've never been in a place this unwelcoming and harsh before. I take in a deep breath.Then I know.I have been here a dozen, a hundred, a thousand hours in a row. Though nothing in it is familiar at this moment, I know the dimensions of the space I am in. I can follow the signs I can't see but know are there. I maneuver myself to a place where there should be solid wall. If I'm wrong, I might fall. I take three giants steps forward, stop with my nose an inch away from the wall I knew would be there.

OK, now. I can negotiate this familiar strange country. I put my back to the wall and scrape along it. I know where I need to go, what I'm heading for. And in a minute or an hour, I am right where I want to be.

My hand traces along a windowsill, and I move my fingers to the handle of the blackened window. I grip it hard, lift with as much muscle as I can.

It slides up like it's tracked on Teflon. My hand goes flying; I could have raised it with just the thought of lifting it.

I am not blinded by the light, though it is a bright day out-side, a perfect sky-mix of cloud and sun. I turn to look at the room. It is the den in our house, where I'd spent count-less hours caring for John, and it was as it always had been. The room is no different than it ever had been. Furniture in place, pictures on the wall where the pictures had been, the dimmer switch near the door turned to where I usually had it set, a notch below center, which gave this room a soothing mellow glow.

Satisfied the room is the room it had always been, I look myself over for any evidence of the surface damage I'd sus-tained crossing it. There is none: no splinters, no cuts, no bruises. I am physically intact, unchanged. Same place, same me in it. I look out the window, then down, making sure there are no more surprises. The drop is what it always had been, and I clamber out and scan across the span of the yard.

John is sitting on the lawn, in the deep comfortable shade of an evergreen elm, a polished ceramic bowl with a kiln-baked pure-white finish held on one knee. He is beautiful. Not the faded version of a big handsome man I hadn't been able to banish from my memory. Now he looks at me whole, healthy, and smiling, but he doesn't say a thing. I smile too, give him a little wave. I want to rush up to him, but do not want to intrude on his obvious joy.

He holds a spoon of heavy Mexican silver, more ornate than any we'd ever owned, in his right hand. He looks me straight in the eyes. I know he loves me. He knows I love him. But this was the closest we could get to one another.

He offers me one last, great, wide smile, then digs his spoon down into the bowl, and raises a perfectly balanced moon of his favorite thing: ice cream. He laughs at the sight, and then I hear him say something he'd said a hundred times before. But I know this is the last time I would ever hear it.

"I'm a happy boy," he says. He rolls the sweet, moon-shaped bite into his mouth and loses himself completely in that infinite pleasure. John looks utterly happy, at peace in the world he had found himself in.

And I know at last that I can carry on my life wholly in this one.

∂∽∾

About Catherine Graves

Catherine Graves is busy raising two children and volunteering for various causes, most recently the Phoenix Children's Hospital Foundation, Florence Crittendon Center for Girls, Barrow's Neurological Institute, and the Craniofacial Foundation of Arizona, among others. She lives in Phoenix with her family. *Checking Out: An In-Depth Look At Losing Your Mind* is her first book.

13259426R00105

Made in the USA
Lexington, KY
21 January 2012